To David Stiller —

Hope you like the book!

TRAIN STORE DIARY

A Romance Novel

by

Robert B. Boeder

Bob Boeder

August 13, 2020

Silverton, CO

1

Railroad Superstition: Never watch a train out of sight if it has a friend on it.

TRAIN STORE DIARY is a mix of fact and fiction based on real events.

Front cover photo by Yvonne Lashmett.

Back cover author photo by Sue Kurtz.

Chapter One

Abby Lindgren had the blues. Standing at the breakfast counter in her pink cotton pajamas, socks, slippers and bathrobe, she nursed her early morning coffee, gazing out her kitchen window at the eastern sky. Not yet risen above Kendall Mountain, the sun washed the undersides of scattered clouds in a soft rosy hue.

Seventies music played softly in the background from her satellite TV-- Anne Murray's honey-dipped voice singing *Snowbird*. Abby wondered, *Should I take Anne Murray's advice? Find someone to fly away with?*

She hadn't slept well again and had been up since five. She wondered if this was all there was to life. Going to work at the Train Store then coming home to an empty house, silent and dark. No friendly lights to greet her, no welcoming noise, no warm cooking smells. After work all she did was sit in her house all by her lonesome listening to her music. *Music is what saves me*, she thought. *Without music I'd be a wreck.*

That's why the first thing she did when she woke up in the morning and when she came home from work was turn on the 1970's music station. She thought she liked 70s music so much because that's the decade when she was born. Her mother had listened to the radio a lot when she was pregnant and Abby must have absorbed the music when she was in her mother's womb. At least, that's what she liked to think.

Music from the 70's was romantic, a balm for her soul and the best of it was sung by women. She loved listening to Linda Ronstadt, Carly Simon, Karen Carpenter, Anne Murray and groups like Queen, Fleetwood Mac and Gladys Knight and the Pips. *Midnight Train to Georgia* was just about her favorite song. Abby didn't know how she'd survive without her music.

This lonely life had not been her plan. She had

married right after college and wanted children, but that had not worked out. That wasn't her fault. Her husband, Carl, ten years older, already had children from a previous marriage and didn't want any more. *Thank God for the Train Store,* Abby thought. *Without that business to go to every day I'd be totally lost.*

Abby lived in Silverton, Colorado, altitude 9,318 feet above sea level. During the week Carl minded their other store in Ouray, twenty miles to the north. He said since the tourist season in the San Juan Mountains lasted for just six months they needed two businesses to make ends meet. She had her Train Store; his store was called Wheels, Wings and Nautical Things. Carl came home on Sundays. He didn't want to commute from Silverton to Ouray over Red Mountain Pass twice a day, so during the week he lived in a trailer next to the Uncompaghre River.

Maybe she should have married someone else with a more exciting job in some exotic locale − an astronaut or a baseball player or an artist, a diplomat, anything other than a retail guy who was absent most of the time.

She needed another living thing to keep her company in the house. She wasn't a cat person. Maybe she should get a dog, an Australian sheepdog, an active animal that would challenge her and get her outside to exercise. Then she remembered. Carl was allergic to dog hair. He broke out in a rash if he came anywhere near a dog.

After finishing her coffee, cereal and breakfast banana, Abby put a bottle of water and a bottle of sweet tea in her lunch bag along with a sandwich bag filled with the trail mix Carl made – M & Ms, peanuts and raisins – a bagel and a container of cream cheese.

Then she showered, bushed her teeth, blow-dried her short blond hair and applied eyebrow pencil and lip gloss. She gave herself a close examination in the bathroom mirror. Not bad, she thought. Flat stomach, firm breasts, hips spreading a little, but no sign of love handles, thank God; a well-preserved figure thanks to not having children. Chin still firm, no sign of doubling up. No turkey neck – at least not yet.

Wrinkle patrol. She touched her forehead. Still smooth. She knew her eyes were the most vulnerable places for wrinkles. Maybe the beginnings of crow's feet at the corners, call them laugh lines, but thank goodness for no dark circles under her eyes. Or rather, thank her Norwegian grandmother for her smooth skin.

That thought led Abby to wonder why Scandinavians have such good skin. Maybe it's because they eat a lot of fish. But not all of them have good skin. Carl's dad Mats was from Sweden and his face was pockmarked.

She didn't bother with makeup or powdering her cheeks. Early 40's, blue eyes, good teeth, healthy, not bad-looking. She could stand to lose five pounds, but so could everyone she knew.

Abby ironed her work clothes – clean jeans and a lavender long-sleeved cotton blouse with a yellow thread sunflower design on the front. She liked the feel of the still-warm clothes on her skin and she wanted to look good for her customers. Abby always wore colored blouses to work. White blouses just got stained or showed the dirt. She wore Nike running shoes. Since she was on her feet all day she needed comfortable footwear with lots of support.

No jewelry, just her gold wedding band. She didn't wear the diamond engagement ring Carl had given her. She worked with her hands framing pictures all day and rings just got in the way.

She couldn't wear the engagement ring even if she wanted to. Carl was a worrier. He worried their businesses would fail and they would go bankrupt. He worried their house would burn down or the roof would cave in during a blizzard. He worried thieves would break in and steal their precious belongings. To make sure Abby's engagement ring was secure, Carl locked it in a safe deposit box at the bank along with their birth certificates, passports and marriage license.

Abby took her lunch bag and checked her purse to make sure she had lip balm, hand lotion and $200 in twenties, tens, fives and ones zipped into a bank envelope – each day's beginning cash for her business. At Silverton's altitude the air was dry. She needed the lip balm and lotion to keep her lips and hands soft.

She locked the door to her house behind her. Silverton was a small town with little to no crime. Some people left their doors unlocked when they went to work, but Carl was a stickler for household security, so Abby made sure all the doors and windows were locked before she left in the morning.

Before setting off she inspected her red 2012 GMC Sierra 1500 V8 pickup. The truck was her pride and joy. She had paid for it herself – $50,000 brand new – and it was loaded. Ebony interior, six-speed automatic transmission, four-wheel-drive, six-speaker audio system, power everything, cruise control, backup camera, heated leather seats, steel wheels, deep tinted glass, fog lights, side steps.

For Abby the truck was a powerful statement of personal and financial independence. Wiping dust off the windshield, she recalled the argument she had with Carl, who drove a Subaru Outback, when she announced her intention to buy a truck.

"I'm going to buy a truck."

"A truck? What for?"

"Lots of reasons."

"Name some."

"I need room in the back to carry stuff around. Like sometimes I need a ladder at work. And I need room to carry cardboard boxes and garbage to the dump. Excuse me, I mean the recycle station."

"Look around. Everybody in Colorado drives Subarus because of the way they handle on our mountain roads with their all-wheel drive."

"The truck I want has four-wheel-drive. If I need a Subaru I'll use yours. Besides, Subarus aren't any good on back country roads because of their low clearance. A truck has high clearance and can go anywhere."

"If you want to drive on back country roads you should get a Jeep."

"Jeeps don't have room to carry stuff. I need a truck."
"Subarus cost half what you'll pay for your truck."

"That doesn't matter. I'm paying for my truck with my own money that I make at my own store."

And that's where the argument ended. The last thing Abby wanted to hear was her husband telling her she couldn't do something. The next day she went to Durango and bought her truck at the GMC dealer. Maybe sometimes, she thought, I do things just to spite Carl.

Abby loved her truck, but most of the time it sat in front of the house, because she also loved her walk to work. After two years the truck had only 8,000 miles on the speedometer; the tires were barely worn. Basically, she drove it to Durango and back for shopping – one hundred miles round trip. The truck was her baby. Abby patted the hood then turned toward town.

Early morning walking was one of the major benefits of living in a small town. Abby didn't have to drive her truck in Silverton. Everything she needed – her business, the bank, post office and grocery store – was within easy walking distance from her home.

Chapter Two

Seven o'clock on a cool, sunny, first Saturday in May. Opening day on the Durango and Silverton Narrow Gauge Railroad. This was the train that brought miners, cowboys and settlers of the Old West into southwestern Colorado over a century ago. Tom Walton was in high spirits for his first trip as engineer. He learned his craft driving diesel locomotives for Amtrak, but running one of the D&SNGRR coal-powered steam locomotives had always been his dream job – and here he was.

The Durango and Silverton Railroad is narrow gauge, also known as slim gauge, running on rails three feet apart as opposed to standard gauge rails which are four feet eight and one-half inches apart. The line was called the Denver and Rio Grande when it was built in 1882 to service gold and silver mines in the remote wilderness of the San Juan Mountains. Round-trip tourist trains between Durango and Silverton began in 1950. By tradition, locomotive 473 powered the first train to

Silverton each season.

Perched on his seat on the right side of the cab facing forward, Tom guided her through the Durango train yard to the coal pile, where eight tons of coal were loaded into the front of the tender then to the water tank, where 5000 gallons poured into the rear of the tender. Then he crept 473, a K-28 class engine built in 1923 by ALCO, the American Locomotive Company, and rebuilt in Durango in 1989, through the yard past the roundhouse to the waiting string of ten vintage passenger cars and one concession car.

Tom brought the engine to a stop, squeezed the grip of the big Johnson Bar facing him into reverse, then waited until he was switched from the yard track onto main track number one. Tugging three shorts on the whistle, the signal that the train is backing up, he gentled the throttle, easing the locomotive backward to couple with the lead passenger car.

The train's conductor Ed Somerset stood alongside the tracks directing Tom in the procedure. It wouldn't do to slam into the coupling. The Durango and Silverton train welcomed passengers from all over the world – Asia, Africa, Europe, Australia, both Americas. The travelers rode in coach cars or open observation cars. Ed Somerset was responsible for the safety of the train and its passengers. He would be unhappy if his precious cargo was knocked off balance by a rude coupling before reaching their seats.

Along with the conductor, engineer and fireman, the rest of the train crew included two brakemen, concession workers and volunteers dressed in period costumes who regaled the passengers with stories about the old days on the train, going back to 1882 when the first rails were laid.

The coupling completed, Engineer Tom pulled two long whistles signaling "Let's Go!" then leaned out his cab window to where he could see Ed Somerset. When

Ed was satisfied all first- day passengers were on the train, he waved his hat and called "All Aboard." Hearing this, Tom looked to his fireman Chase Bigelow for his sign the engine was ready to go to work.

Chase was a young man from a wealthy West Texas oil family who grew up infatuated with everything about steam trains. Ever since he was a little kid and his parents brought him to Durango to ride the train his ambition was to be an engineer. He idolized Tom Walton and the others who drove the D&SNGRR steam locomotives to Silverton. His ambition was to join them, but for now he was a fireman. Chase released a stream of condensed water from the engine cylinders, then yelled "Highball," the all-clear signal.

With the bell ringing, Tom Walton tugged the whistle cord two shorts to indicate the train was moving. He pushed the throttle ahead and the train lurched forward, rolling slowly at first out of the yard, behind the Strater Hotel, across College Drive, then picking up speed along Narrow Gauge Avenue, past the backs of businesses through downtown Durango.

Approaching each intersection, Tom pulled two longs followed by one short and another long signaling for traffic to stop, the train was coming. Once the train crossed the steel plate girder 15th Street Bridge over the Animas River, (*Rio de las Animas Perdidas,* the River of Lost Souls), in full spate now with snow melt, it was out of the main congested downtown area and Tom could pick up speed.

Fireman was a young man's job and Tom had complete confidence in Chase Bigelow. Chase wore gauntlet gloves and long sleeves to protect his hands and arms from sparks. Every few minutes he stepped down on the lever releasing the firebox door, then he tossed in four or five shovels of coal. He had learned to read the fire in order to balance the draft and slope the fire bed for maximum efficiency. Chase kept an eye on the water glass pressure gauge making sure it was between

175 and 200. He also kept his work area clean, hosing down the cab with hot water to wash coal dust out the open back and sides. Then he directed the hose onto the coal still in the tender to keep the dust down.

Driving the steam train to Silverton was a total sensory overload for the engineer and the fireman between the noise from sitting right behind the engine, the heat from the firebox every time Chase opened the door, the shaking of the locomotive from the pistons banging up and down and the swaying of the train from the bumpy unevenness of the tracks − to say nothing of the visuals of the beautiful San Juan Mountains and the spectacular Animas River Canyon the train ran through. It was a bumpy ride, but from that day forward Tom swore he would never tire of controlling the living breathing beast that was the number 473 locomotive.

For most of the forty-five miles to Silverton the three-foot-wide narrow gauge tracks followed the Animas River north from Durango. A patrolman in a pop car ran ahead of the train to clear rocks and other debris from the tracks. Tom highballed the engine and cars through the U-shaped river valley, dug out by glaciers millions of years ago. Passengers exclaimed at a herd of elk grazing on the river bank. The train passed the Animas Valley Falls, crossed over Hermosa Creek and rolled across Highway 550 where cars paused, halted by blinking red barriers. Some people got out of their cars to wave and take pictures as the train passed by.

Then the engine huffed and puffed as it pulled the train up Hermosa Hill on the north side of the valley. After passing under the Highway 550 Bridge Tom took the train through the Shalona Meadows on its way to the village of Rockwood.

Departing Rockwood, 473 passed between the red granite walls of the Rockwood Cut and approached the twin curves of the High Line, the narrowest and most dramatic section of the railroad that had been blasted with black powder out of a vertical cliff on the north side of the river. Tom slowed the train through the Horseshoe Curve for safety and for the passengers to have time to take all the photos they wanted.

With 473's wheel flanges squeaking and groaning in his ears and the rails inches from the edge of the cliff, Tom peered back over his shoulder to make sure all eleven cars were still behind him and to watch the riders leaning out of their windows to take in the spectacular scene of the Animas River tumbling through its gorge two hundred forty feet below.

Leaving the High Line, the train crossed the Animas on a wrought-iron high bridge where Chase opened the blow-off cocks, forcing mud and other trash out of the boiler on either side of the engine. On this sunny morning, passengers oohed and aahed over the spectacular rainbow this created.

A few miles to the north Tom took a drink from the water bottle at his elbow as he guided 473 past the

Tacoma power plant on the opposite side of the Animas from the tracks. Tacoma was where a flash flood had once widened the river bed and tore out twenty-two miles of track. The power plant was fed by water from Electra Lake, a man-made reservoir on Elbert Creek.

Then, in a little over a mile, they passed the former Ah Wilderness dude ranch, closed since 1986. Tom moved on another half mile, where he pulled one short blast on the whistle before halting the train at Tank Creek, half way to Silverton, the first of two stops to take on water.

Chapter Three

Springtime in Silverton − the air cool and dry, the sun shining in a partly cloudy sky. Abby lived across a graveled street from a line of single-wide trailers. Her walk took her up the alley behind her house past an empty lot, then she turned right on 17th street to Greene, the only paved street in Silverton, across the bridge over Cement Creek, past the archives, Mining Museum and the San Juan County courthouse with its freshly mowed lawn on her right and the town hall on her left. She crossed Greene to the sunny side of the street, passed some shops, crossed 13th and saw her best friend, Yvonne Fletcher, sitting in the sun on the metal bench in front of My Things, Yvonne's women's clothing store next to Abby's Train Store.

Every woman needs one friend, a confidante who knows her like a book, the one who can tell whether she's lost or gained a single pound that week, whether she's in an up or down mood that day and what clothes look just right on her. Yvonne was that person for Abby. Abby could always count on Yvonne being honest with her – straight up, supportive and positive, never mean or critical.

"Hi dear," Abby greeted her friend. "Charging your batteries?"

Yvonne had thick brown hair with red overtones. She was large, generously proportioned, but with a delicate facial structure, high cheek bones, wide-spaced brown eye, a straight nose, full lips, perfect teeth and a big smile. Abby thought she was beautiful.

"I love the sun," Yvonne said. "Preparing for the big day. First train's on the way. You look good today."

"Thanks. I'm kind of in a funk."

"Tell Auntie Yvonne all about it." Yvonne was the same age as Abby, divorced with no kids.

"I should be happy, looking forward to the train coming, a new season welcoming tourists to Silverton and making money in the store, but my heart just isn't in it."

"Cheer up, Abby. For goodness sake. What's the problem?"

"I'm lonely. During the day I'm fine because I'm with people in the store or I can talk to you, but when I go home after work it's like a morgue. You know what I've started doing?"

"Tell me."

"I've started writing Post-its to myself and sticking them on the bathroom wall in the store. Like, 'You're wonderful. Enjoy the sunny day' and 'Have a good day. Love you, Sweetpea.' Just to pick myself up. It's pathetic. The only thing that saves me is listening to my music on the radio."

"What about Carl? Does he call during the week? Do you chat online? Communicate in any way?"

"Not really. If he's tied up or going to be late on Sunday he'll call, or if there's a business issue, but otherwise no."

"Email?"

"He doesn't like emailing."

"Texting?"

"We don't text. I have a smartphone. He doesn't."

"Hmmmm. Sounds like a communication breakdown. How many years have you had your store?"

"Fourteen. We came here fourteen years ago."

"And how many years have you been married?"

"Sixteen. Seems like forever."

"If it was seven I'd say you had the seven-year itch. Maybe there's a fourteen-year itch you have to scratch twice as hard as the seven-year one."

"Maybe." Abby looked at her watch. "Almost ten. I've got to open up. I'll talk to you later."

Chapter Four

Tom brought the train to a halt at the Tank Creek water stop, then pulled one long and three shorts, the signal to protect the rear of the train. When the train came to a stop the brakeman got off carrying his red box flagging kit and walked down the tracks. The kit contained red flags and flares that were used to warn an approaching train or pop car that a train was stopped ahead.

Tom and his fireman dismounted from the locomotive cab. While Tom oiled the driver wheels and their connecting rods, Chase pulled down the water spout to refill the tender. Conductor Ed Somerset joined them to stretch his legs.

"How you boys doin?" Ed asked.

"Just fine, Ed," Tom said. "How's everything back in the cars?"

"No problems. Pretty day. Everybody's enjoying the ride."

Ed performed a quick inspection of the brake rigging and wheel assemblies under the coaches then boarded the train. Their labors finished, Tom and Chase stepped up into the cab, where Tom signaled the brakeman to return to the train with five long blasts. When the brakeman indicated he was back on board, Chase gave Tom the "Highball" signal. It seemed like the locomotive drew fresh energy from its long drink of water. After two short whistles 473 leapt ahead, eager to be off again.

In short order the train passed Tall Timber Resort, accessible only by train or helicopter where guests paid $1000 a day to be pampered in the wilderness. Tall Timber is in an open valley, a kind of park where in 1951 the movie *Denver and Rio Grande* was filmed. The climax of the movie was a spectacular head-on collision and destruction of two Denver & Rio Grande

Western locomotives, numbers 319 and 345.

With Tall Timbers behind him Tom guided the train across Grasshopper Creek, its banks lined with blue spruce, the Colorado state tree, to Cascade Canyon. A wye in Cascade Canyon was where the winter trains turned around and headed back to Durango. Today 473 sauntered past the wye and crossed the Animas River once again on a wrought-iron bridge.

As he filled his shovel with coal, Chase looked out the open end of the cab to the northeast and marveled at the high peaks and jagged beauty of the Needle Mountains. Next,Tom brought the train into the Needle Creek Valley, pulled one short whistle and stopped to take on water at the Needleton tank.

Needleton was where mountain climbers got off the baggage car with their gear, crossed the Animas River on a footbridge and hiked into Chicago Basin, where they challenged three fourteeners − Mount Eolus,

Windom Peak and Sunshine Peak. No one disembarked that day. Chicago Basin was still full of snow. May was too early in the year for mountain climbing.

When Chase finished filling the tender tank he signaled "Highball" to Tom who gave two short blasts and the train moved forward battling its way up the canyon past Ruby, No Name and Tenmile Creeks toward the spectacular Grenadier Range to the northeast. Tom admired the aspen and Engelmann spruce trees marching up the surrounding mountainsides, scarred in places by avalanche slides. Heavy snow and avalanches were two reasons the train didn't run to Silverton in the winter. Another reason was the lack of tourist interest in going to Silverton when the temperatures were below freezing and few shops were open.

Exactly ten miles from Silverton, Tenmile Creek iss the site of a station on the old toll road between Durango and Silverton. It's also the place with the steepest grade on the journey. For most of the trip the grade is 2.5%, but around Tenmile Creek the grade grows to 3% and 4% in one short section. At that point Chase increased the pace of his coal shoveling to keep the engine at full throttle.

For the next seven miles the tracks crossed the paths of numerous snow slides. Tom didn't have to worry about them, but back when the train served Silverton year-round the tracks had to be kept clear of snow. This required the railroad to hire out-of-work miners in Silverton to do the shoveling. Occasionally, an avalanche was so deep the shovelers resorted to hacking tunnels through the snow rather than going to all the trouble of entirely clearing the tracks. At one point a 400-foot snow shed was erected to shelter the tracks, but it had since burned down. History doesn't reveal if the destruction of the snow shed was intentional, accidental or sabotage.

Tom eased the train across the Animas on a 220 foot steel deck plate girder bridge, passed over Elk Creek and entered Elk Park, where there was a siding and a wye. Elk Park was also a flag stop for fishermen and backpackers hiking the 486 mile Colorado Trail from Durango to Denver that follows Elk Creek eastward. Elk Park was full of dandelions − a favorite spring food for the deer, elk and bears that favor the San Juan Mountains.

Chase looked off to his right for a good view of Mount Garfield as the train passed the Molas Creek footbridge, used by Colorado Trail hikers. From there to Silverton hundreds of mine dumps on the mountain sides on both sides of the river offered evidence of the intense mining activity that constituted a large part of Silverton's heritage.

473 steamed over the Animas one last time with the remains of the Champion Mine on the west side of the track, then crossed Mineral Creek. The train passed the yellow wood-frame Silverton Welcome Center alongside the wye, where it would reverse directions for

the return trip to Durango. Tom pulled one long whistle for approaching station as he came to a siding where unused freight cars were parked and the Silverton Depot came into view at the end of 10th Street on Chase's left side of the train. The D & S railroad agent wearing a conductor's hat stood outside the depot and waved as the train went by.

Tom brought the train around the final bend and merged with 12th Street as he began applying the brakes up to Blair where 473 came to a halt. Tom felt like he had just entered a 19th century mining town with Victorian-era buildings in front of him and mine dumps littering the mountainsides on all sides. He smiled and waved at celebrants dressed in period costumes greeting the first train of the season.

Turning to Chase, Tom said, "Good job, Fireman. That was a thrill. Can't wait to take her back to Durango."

"Thanks Mr. Engineer. Looks like we're got a

reception committee waiting for us.   We're celebrities –
at least for a few minutes."

Chapter Five

The Train Store was a place where old men regaled
young boys with stories about what it was like to drive a
steam engine and how much fun it had been to sit
around a hot stove in the caboose drinking whiskey and
telling tales as their freight train hurtled through the
night. The store was where retirees were reminded of
how great it had been to work for a railroad before all
the mergers turned the train industry into a corporate
strait-jacket. Riding the D&SNGRR was a trip down
memory lane for steam train buffs and Abby wanted her
store to reflect that feeling.

Abby unlocked the old-fashioned double front doors
of the store and propped them open. An open door
invited customers to come in. Even though she had two
"Open" signs in her windows, Abby had found that
people walked right on by if she left the doors closed.
Then she went into the back room and flipped the
breaker switches that turned on the lights.

The building housing the store was the second oldest wood frame structure in Silverton, built in 1875. Originally, the space was occupied by a mercantile store then it became the *Silverton Standard* newspaper office. The printing machines were still in the back room. The toilet didn't work very well and there was no central heating. In the summer, at 9318 feet, the solar heat coming in the big front windows in the morning was all the store needed to warm up from the overnight chill. In cold weather Abby used three electric space heaters and a pellet burning stove to heat the place.

The front of the building was painted bright yellow with the words "Railroad Art by Scotty" emblazoned in red above the windows. The idea for the store came from Carl's childhood friend Herschel Scott, aka Scotty. Carl and Scotty grew up together in Salinas, California, where Scotty honed his artistic talent creating drawings of train locomotives and cabooses using a technique called stippling or *pointillism*. Scotty worked through a magnifying glass and used a special technical drawing pen to make his pictures with tiny dots of ink. He also used a computer to produce railroad-related posters in the 1930s art deco style.

After a hitch in the Air Force Scotty decided to devote himself full-time to his art, but he needed a gallery where he could sell it. He also needed a businessman to help him. He knew Carl Lindgren had an entrepreneurial streak, so the two of them got together and opened their first store in the tourist town of Leavenworth, Washington. That's where Abby and Carl met.

Scotty was as restless as the prairie wind. He couldn't stay in one place for long and the Leavenworth store wasn't doing as well as Carl liked, so they moved to Silverton, the northern terminus of the D&SNGRR. Scotty and Carl figured Silverton would be a good place to sell train art – and they were right.

Abby put the bagel and cream cheese in a small

refrigerator she had in back of the store alongside a microwave oven where she warmed them up. She put the water, sweet tea and trail mix for snacking on her work table. She turned on the cash register and placed the twenty, ten, five and one dollar bills in their slots, then she turned on the radio tuned to KSJC, the local radio station.

Whether at home or at work Abby hated silence, so she always either had the radio on or activated the CD player she kept in the store loaded with train-related music. Donna Summer was singing *Bad Girls* on KSJC and Abby joined in on the chorus. Music was one of the things that brought her out of her early morning funk.

Train store customers, especially the women, also brightened Abby's outlook on life. She tried to greet every one of them with a smile and a friendly welcome.

Just then a woman came into the store. "Hi, how're you doing today?" Abby said.

Like most customers, the woman returned Abby's smile and responded enthusiastically with, "Very well, thanks. And how are you?"

"I'm just great. Let me know if I can help you with anything."

"Thanks. I'm waiting for the train to get here."

"So am I," Abby said. "Eleven thirty. Won't be long. Another thirty minutes."

Like this woman, most of Abby's American customers were pleased to be on vacation in Silverton and especially happy to be shopping. She preferred single woman customers, but loved it when two women came in together, because they would encourage each other to buy stuff. She related better to her women customers than the men. The men could be difficult because they assumed because she was a woman she knew nothing about railroads, but over the years Abby had gained considerable train knowledge and was capable of impressing her male customers when she was in the mood, which wasn't every day.

The retail business, at least in Silverton, often boiled down to the fact that women wanted to spend money and men didn't. How many times, Abby asked herself, had a couple come into the store, the woman would see something she liked or thought her man would like and she would say, "Bill, come look at this." Bill would come over reluctantly. She would say, "Do you like this?" He would reply grumpily, "No!", and they would walk out without buying anything.

The D&SNG train attracted riders from all over the world. Abby could always tell when Europeans came into the store, not from their clothing since everyone dressed alike, but because, unlike the Americans, they didn't return her greeting. Some didn't speak English. Others, especially the British, were shy at first, but when she asked where they were from and got them talking, they wouldn't shut up. Many of the Brits were members of steam engine clubs and regaled Abby with pictures on their phones of various steam-powered vehicles they owned.

Of all the foreigners she liked French people the most and Dutch men the least. Dutch women were nice, but the men were always looking for a deal, offering less than her marked prices. Although the French were the least likely to speak English they were the most effervescent, bubbling over with happiness at being in such a beautiful mountain town as Silverton. For the Europeans, Silverton was exactly what they were looking for on their holidays – a late 19th century American West town preserved in amber.

Most of the Americans who came in the store were average tourists, but Abby could tell the ones who had money. The women dressed in brand new shorts and blouses – vacation outfits that belonged in places like La Jolla or Palm Springs rather than in a rugged mountain town like Silverton. Abby thought the men in their golf shorts and Ralph Lauren Polo shirts looked silly. Few Silverton men wore shorts, even in the summer. And the wealthy ones never bought anything. They already had two of everything they wanted or needed so they just came in the store to kill time before the train left. The women wore expensive rings and bracelets and looked bored, like they couldn't wait to leave this quaint but dusty place.

Abby couldn't decide if she was jealous of those women. She noticed them because she had grown up poor and always wondered what it would be like to have money. Did she want to be like the women with the pricey bracelets? She didn't know. She was ambivalent.

She did notice the sports cars that drove up Highway 550 in groups and stopped in Silverton for lunch. She told herself she wouldn't mind having a nice red BMW to show off to Yvonne.

Just then Abby heard the familiar one long blast of a whistle signaling the train's arrival in town. The store was empty of customers, so she put on her engineer's cap, turned the radio off, taped her "Be Right Back" sign on the window, locked the door and hurried down Greene Street past souvenir and gift stores, Fetch's T-shirt shop and the Grand Imperial Hotel where Lacey Black was warming up on the piano, to 12th Street then she turned left past the bank on the corner to Blair Street, where the train stopped and passengers got off. The weather was cool and sunny; the atmosphere was festive. Townspeople dressed in Victorian era costumes were gathered to welcome the first train of the season as Silverton Brass Band members tuned up their instruments across the street from the end of the tracks.

In a few minutes locomotive 473 came around the corner into view, flags flying, and the Brass Band struck up *The Washington Post March* by John Philip Sousa. The music energized the colorful crowd of spectators who greeted the passengers and train crew enthusiastically. Miss Kitty, a local legend costumed as a saloon girl, strutted in front of the engine pumping her umbrella up and down.

"Hooray for the first train of the year!" bellowed Benson Bernie, standing next to Abby. So-called because he rented a room at the Benson Hotel, Bernie, a white- bearded older gentleman, wore a grey top hat and a tailored, charcoal colored, knee-length frock coat with a fancy double-breasted black vest, fitted full-front grey trousers and a lavish purple cravat with a pearl stickpin tucked into the neck of his white silk shirt.

"You look terrific, Bernie," Abby said. "Does your shirt have cufflinks?"

"Thank you, ma'am," Bernie replied, shooting the cuffs of his shirt to show Abby his cufflinks. "Genuine pearls. I always dress to fit the occasion."
Engineer Tom Walton and his fireman, Chase Bigelow, swung down from the cab and were instantly

surrounded in front of the engine, obliging passengers with photos. Although she didn't know him, Abby thought the engineer looked handsome as he grinned for the photographers. Standing in front of the crowd waving, Abby smiled at the engineer. She felt their eyes touch.

"I like your cap, girl," Tom shouted, beaming at her.

"I like yours too," Abby yelled back with a wave, thinking, *My, but he's got a warm smile.*

Passengers streamed off the train heading for Greene Street. They only had two hours in town, barely enough time for lunch and some shopping.

Chapter Six

Abby hurried back to the Train Store, removed the "Be Right Back" sign, opened both front doors again, went behind her work table and turned the radio back on. *Blue Clear Sky,* a George Strait song, was playing. Abby liked country music almost as much as she liked 70s music.

Her work table stood in the middle of the store facing the front doors so she could greet people as they entered. On her right was a counter with the cash register, credit card machine and telephone. On her left was another counter full of eight by ten train prints divided according to individual railroads.

Standing behind her work table, framing Scotty's prints and posters was Abby's main job. She took pleasure in working with her hands, assembling the pictures. Sometimes her mind wandered and she would make a mistake like forgetting to put the glass in before she nailed the mat to the frame with framer's points, but she could always rectify her error. The hardest or maybe the most aggravating part of framing a picture was getting the class clean. There always seemed to be a speck she missed and she had to go over and over it to make sure both sides were clean.

In front of her were her work tools – glue gun, Scotch tape, stapler, scissors, glass cleaner spray, hand lotion, knife, "Train Store" stamp, glass brush, surgical tape, screwdrivers and pliers, double-sided tape, packaging tape. Arrayed on shelves around her were framing mats in three colors – marble, green and blue – cut in various sizes and configurations; wood frames in several different sizes already assembled; metal frames she put together herself; and the pieces of glass she cut to fit the frames. Behind her was a pellet-burning stove. At her feet was an electric space heater. Two other space heaters were placed in the rear corners of the store.

The side walls of the store, painted yellow, were

covered with framed train prints, mainly locomotives and cabooses, of various railroads, along with maps of the territory they traversed. The rear wall was devoted to framed posters of railroads, vintage streetcars, World War II airplanes, vintage cars, and train-connected national parks, plus Colorado and California – themed tourist destinations. All prints and posters were created by Scotty. The guy had been immensely productive and creative. Unframed posters of the same subjects in two sizes, eight by ten and twelve by eighteen, were displayed on racks in the front of the store and in boxes along the walls. Ceiling lights illuminated the framed pictures and posters.

One front corner of the store featured shelves loaded with kids' toy trains, toy airplanes and plane and train-related shopping bags for sale. Boxes full of bandanas, rail spikes, spike whistles, engineer hats, train t-shirts and date nails sat on the tops of wood shipping crates placed against the side walls.

The date nails were relics of earlier times that

functioned as maintenance records. Two-digit numbers on the heads of the nails corresponded to the years maintenance crews installed anything made of wood on the railroad – rail ties mostly, but also bridges and water tanks. Some people collected date nails and Abby was happy to sell them for a dollar each.

Abby also sold metal train-related signs. One of them, the "Do Not Hump" sign, was a customer favorite. Do Not Hump meant whatever the customer wanted it to mean. College girls bought them for their dorm rooms. In fact, Do Not Hump was a real train phrase related to forming trains in railroad marshalling yards. In each marshalling yard there was a small hill or hump. The yard engine pushed individual cars over the hump and gravity carried them to their respective trains, where they coupled with a crash. Do Not Hump signs were placed on cars carrying fragile items likely to be damaged in the normal coupling process. Seeing the signs, the engineers knew they were to avoid humping those cars and instead gently push them to their trains, where they would couple less violently.

Abby didn't limit herself to train signs. She sold other signs designed to appeal to her customers' sense of humor. One of them was a picture of John Wayne dressed in cowboy hat and red bandana with his advice "Never Apologize and Never Explain. It's a Sign of Weakness". Her favorite was a picture of Wonder Woman with the observation, "I'm not saying I'm Wonder Woman. I'm just saying no one has seen the two of us in a room together." The best-selling sign was "Co-Pilot Check List: Don't Touch Anything. Keep Your Mouth Shut."

In one corner of her store Abby sold airplane-related items – framed pictures of World War II bombers and fighter planes, bumper stickers with sayings like "Kiss a Pilot" and "Real Airplanes Have Round Engines" plus replica propellers of World War I airplanes like the Sopwith Camel. She told customers that no home should be without a propeller above the fireplace. The replica propellers were expensive – over $200, but she managed to sell one every month.

Abby's small train museum sat on a platform above the airplane display – mostly old oil cans and antique lanterns used for signaling purposes. These items gave the store an old-timey ambiance and were not for sale.

After the passengers disembarked the train backed down to the wye at the south end of town next to the visitor's center, where the crew turned the train around and ate lunch. The crew waited about an hour before backing the train into town again in preparation for departure.

For various reasons train management discouraged crew members from venturing into the town business district, but sometimes they slipped away to go shopping or visit friends. Occasionally they came in the Train Store. After fourteen years Abby knew most of the crew members and was able to greet them by name. She carried D&SNGRR-related pins, posters and prints and gave train crews ten percent discounts on their purchases.

Customers seemed to come in the Train Store in waves. The store would fill up with shoppers and Abby would be busy for twenty minutes selling things to people lined up at the cash register. Then they would all clear out and there would be a trough, a few minutes of quiet before the store would fill up again.

The store was entering a wave phase, filling up with customers. Abby stopped what she was doing to attend to their needs.

"Where are your pins?" a young girl wanted to know.

"Right there in the glass case," Abby said, pointing behind her. She sold over four hundred different railroad pins. "Five fifty each. That includes the tax. There'll be a number under the pin. If you want one, give me the number and I'll find it in these drawers over here."

She pointed to a case with four-hundred twenty-five
small drawers full of pins.

"Do you have a pin for the Durango and Silverton
Railroad?" The girl was standing in front of the glass
case.

Abby moved to the back of the case. "Yes, it's right
here." She pointed at the pin. "The orange one.
Number sixty-nine. The Silverton pin is right next to it
with a steam locomotive on a white background."

"I'll take one of each."

At the cash register Abby said, "That will be eleven
dollars. Cash or charge?"

The girl dug a roll of bills out of her purse. "I'll pay
cash and I want to buy a bag of these Engineer Gummi
Bears too."

"The Gummi Bears are $2.49, made special for the Train Store," Abby smiled. "Double the sugar of normal Gummi Bears."

"Really?"

"No. I'm just teasing you."

As Abby was putting the pins and the candy in a bag and making change for the girl a line was forming at the cash register. Abby was superstitious. When the first customer of the day bought something she believed it was a sign that would be a good day. The next half hour she was kept busy by customers buying train stuff. Most of the purchases were small – between five and twenty dollars – and reflected the tourist's desire for mementos to remember their train ride.

When Abby had time to look up from the cash register she noticed a tall, good-looking, broad shouldered fellow enter the store. He was dressed in dark blue bib overalls, a light blue work shirt with a blue bandana tied around his neck, an engineer's hat and work boots with his work gloves stuck in his back pocket. It was the man she had exchanged looks with when the train arrived that morning – the locomotive 473 engineer. Most of Abby's customers had ridden the train to Silverton and knew who he was. He commanded their respect, but in a friendly way. They made room for him as he came toward her.

"Well, hello," she greeted him with special music in her voice. "Welcome to the Train Store. I saw you having your picture taken."

"Hi," the man approached her. Their eyes locked. His were an unusual color – cobalt blue – and set wide in his lean, handsome face – high cheek bones, a straight nose and a well-shaped mouth with a hint of sensuality. He took off his hat with one hand, smiled and extended the other.

There's that smile again, Abby thought. Warm and deep.

"I'm Tom Walton. Pleased to meet you."

He had wavy dark brown hair and was a couple of inches taller than Abby. She liked that.

Abby took his hand in hers and returned his smile. "Hello. Nice to meet you. I'm Abby Lindgren."

Abby's nails weren't manicured. Her hands weren't soft. They were dry and rough from years of framing pictures. They were working hands, just like his.

Tom Walton's hand pressure was just right – not a limp rag and not a crushing grip. Their hands fit together perfectly. She let him hold hers for a few seconds longer than a normal hand shake.

"You've got a cool store here. Creaky floors." The

Train Store still had its original wood floor cut from Engelmann spruce. The floor squeaked when walked on.

"Thanks. No one can sneak up on me."

He smiled at her joke. "When was it built?"

"Eighteen seventy-five. Single story, wood frame. It sits right on the ground. You can feel the floor is slanted slightly downhill in the front corner. It's the oldest commercial building in town. Are you new with the railroad? I thought I knew most of the crew members."

"This is my first run with the D and S. I was an Amtrak engineer for twenty years, but their trains are so computerized driving them is no fun anymore. Plus, I got tired of working for a corporation. The bottom line is all they think about. There's no real human connection. Working for the D & S has always been my dream. I jumped at the chance to pilot this train. It's the best steam railroad in the country and probably the world. I'm only half way through my first run but I already feel at home."

Abby loved the sound of Tom Walton's voice, rich and deep like a church organ. As he talked Abby was drawn into his aura. She looked at his hands and wondered how they would feel caressing her body. Then she melted into his eyes and felt her life change. She couldn't help herself.

"Are you married?" she blurted out, blushing.

"No. I'm a widower. My wife passed away a year ago. That's another reason I signed on with the D & S. Move to Durango for a fresh start."

A woman was waiting behind Tom to buy a jigsaw puzzle. She had a frown on her face. Abby ignored her. It was like she and Tom were the only people on the planet.

"I'm sorry about your wife."

Just then four long whistles echoed off the mountainsides surrounding Silverton, the sign passengers had ten minutes to board.

Tired of waiting for Abby to take her money, the woman returned the jigsaw puzzle to its rack and walked out of the store.

Tom said, "I left my fireman in charge. That's his signal for me to get back to the train. It's been a pleasure." He put his engineer's hat on and reached out to grip Abby's hand again.

She took his hand and didn't want to let go. "Likewise," was all she could manage to say. Then, as Tom walked out the door, "Come back."

Abby kept a diary at the store. It was a small memo book with a brown cover, three inches by five inches.

No one knew about the diary – not even Yvonne. Abby kept it hidden in the back of the top drawer of a filing cabinet full of train prints and route maps that stood next to her work station. The diary was private, blind to the future, written in the moment, for Abby's eyes only. Normally, she filled its pages with observations about the weather or unusual train-related events. Until that day she had rarely confided her true feelings in writing.

In the late afternoon when all her customers had left the store, *I Want to Know What Love Is* by Foreigner was playing on the radio. Abby wrote, "Diary entry for 5-6-14. First day of the train season. Met a new engineer and I've already got a crush on him. Am I being rash? Foolish? Maybe, but I don't care. How many chances for happiness does each of us have in our lives? One? Two if we're lucky? I'm grabbing this one."

Chapter Seven

Walking down Greene Street the next morning, Abby looked up at a band of color crossing the lower slopes of Sultan Mountain west of town, parallel to Highway 550. She felt like she had been reborn. Yvonne was sitting in the sun in front of her store as usual waiting for her. Yvonne greeted her friend with a version of a verse from *City of New Orleans*, her favorite train song. "Good mornin, Miss Abby. How are ya?"

Abby sang back, "Don't cha know me? I'm yer native daughter."

The two shared a laugh. Yvonne was surprised by what her friend was wearing.

"Look at you," she said, a big grin on her face. "It's 9:30. You're earlier than usual. And aren't you the classy dame? Wearing a dress!"

Abby rarely wore a dress to work. She always wore jeans because jeans went better with Silverton, with what she was selling and they didn't show dirt. Keeping the doors open meant dust blew into the store from the street. Despite her best efforts to keep the place clean, at the end of the day everything in the store – including Abby herself – was covered with a thin film of dust.

"A sun-dress with a beautiful purple floral pattern," Yvonne continued. "You look great. Are you going to play tennis? And is that a whiff of perfume I'm getting?"

Abby never wore scent to work, but this morning she had sprayed some on.

"I love your perfume. What is it?"
"Coco by Chanel."

"Can I have some?"

"Are you serious? No. It's mine."

"I'm always serious. You know that. If you won't let me use yours I'll just get some of my own at one of the boutique shops in downtown Durango. What's the occasion?"

"I'm here early because I was antsy. I couldn't stay home any longer. The occasion is the arrival of the train."

"What's so special about that? The train comes every day in the summer. Next month there'll be two trains a day, then three and even four in July."

"It's not just the arrival of the train. It's who's going to be driving it."

"You know more about that than I do. Who's the engineer?"

"It's a new guy named Tom Walton. Wavy dark brown hair and he has the bluest eyes I've ever seen. They're deep blue. Cobalt blue. I've fallen in love."

"You're kidding."

"I'm serious. At least I think I am. I fell in love with him the first time I saw him. It was when he and his fireman were posing for pictures yesterday in front of the locomotive. Our eyes met. He said he liked my hat, I said I liked his — and that was it. Later he came in the store and we talked. Not for long, but he told me his wife died last year and he's always wanted to be an engineer on the Durango and Silverton train."

"Sounds like a normal conversation with a train guy, but this time you fell in love."

"It was like the best first date of my life."

"I've always thought of locomotive driver as a romantic occupation."

"You got that right. Especially if you own a train store. There's lots of great songs written about trains. Trains can be romantic, taking people on long journeys to exotic places."

"Like Silverton?"

"Yes. People come here to get married all the time."

"Just kidding."

"D'you mind if I change the subject?"
"Go ahead."

"Did I ever tell you I write Post-its to myself and stick them on the bathroom wall?"

"That's a little weird. If I'm depressed in the morning I have to remember to smile. A few customers spending their money makes me feel better. Tell me more about your Post-its."

"It's to give me a positive message. Today I put one up about Tom Walton. 'I feel sunny when I think of you.' It's just a small thing, but Post-its lift my spirits when I'm down in the dumps."

"Whatever works is fine with me. How did you fall in love with this guy?"

"It was love at first sight."

"Really?"

"Yes. It happens all the time."

"Of course it does. It might be the rule rather than the exception. But people fall in love gradually too."

"I think that's what happened with me and Carl. I fell in love with him gradually. I had to kind of talk myself into it. I thought I needed a man to hang onto − someone to support me. I didn't have the self-confidence to be on my own that I have now. I should have realized that and moved on at some point, but up until now I haven't been brave enough."

"Speaking of Carl, how did the two of you get together?"

"You want the story of my life?"
"Sure. Why not?"

"I grew up poor in Oakland, California. My parents were working class people. I had an older brother, Dave, who joined the Air Force right after high school. He's stationed all over the country. I don't see him very often.

We lived across the bay from San Francisco – sophisticated, wealthy, unobtainable – or so I thought at the time. I dreamed of meeting someone from that world, but I couldn't get into Stanford or Cal Berkeley. I decided to leave town and enrolled at a community college in Seattle. When I graduated I went to Leavenworth, Washington, looking for a job. It's a tourist town like Silverton. I met Carl there and went to work for him at his train store."

"Was that store like this one?"

"It was just like this one. The artist, Carl's friend, Herschel Scott, was a stickler for details. He insisted on everything being the same. Looking back, I was in love with the idea of being in love. I was in my 20s. All my friends were getting married. One thing led to another and Carl and I wound up getting married. I thought that's what came next after college."

"It doesn't have to follow automatically, but when you're 21-years-old that's what it feels like."

"I didn't want to be left behind. I dreamed of marrying someone exciting from the elite San Francisco world, but I got Carl instead – ambitious, hard-working and dull."

"What are you going to do about him now that you're in love with someone else?"

"I haven't given it any thought. It's too early. I'll think of something."

"So what's it feel like? Love at first sight."

"I think I was so stunned I didn't realize I was in love with Tom that moment at the train or even when he came into the store. It was this morning when it hit me. I woke up and I wasn't depressed. I was happy and when I asked myself why it was obvious. I'd met this guy and we connected. The way he looked at me, the way he talked to me. It's like I stopped getting older. I was in love with him. My world changed; my eyes changed. The sun's brighter. The air's fresher. The water's sweeter."

"What about the tourists? Are they going to be richer and happier to spend more money in the train store?"

"I don't know. Maybe. Most of them are glad to be on vacation in Silverton so they can't get much happier. If they see that I'm happy maybe that will loosen their purse strings. The ordinary parts of my life are special now. Love's made them that way."

"Wow. I wish I could bring some of that feeling into my life. What if he doesn't reciprocate?"

"I'll just have to wait and see if he comes in the store again. If he does, I'll turn on the charm, fire up my personality, blind him with my smile. If he comes back, one look will tell me if I've got him. It's either there or it isn't. Know what I mean? I'll know if he reciprocates. I've got to go to work. See you later."

When she first opened her store, Abby had noticed people from other parts of the country who came in were often confused about what time it was and when they should return to the train. To help them she placed four clocks on the wall of the store across the aisle from where she stood at the cash register. Each clock was set to a different U.S. time zone – Eastern, Central, Mountain and Pacific.

That day Abby kept her eye on the Mountain Time clock – Silverton time. When the hands reached one thirty, she thought, *If he's coming it will be in the next fifteen minutes*. Time crawled like a glacier. When she heard four long whistles, the signal for passengers to return to the train, she knew her time was up. Tom Walton wasn't coming in the Train Store that day.

Diary entry for 5-7-14. "The Bible says, 'Love bears all things, believes all things, hopes all things, endures all things. Love never ends.' He didn't show up today, but he'll be back – and he won't have a chance or a choice. I'm going to make him love me."

Chapter Eight

The next day Abby was back in her jeans wearing her favorite blouse – yellow and long-sleeved with a red lariat design embroidered around the neck. Wanting to smell nice for her man, she had put on perfume. Yvonne was inside My Things helping customers when Abby came to work. They didn't have their normal gossip session. She opened up and went through her usual routine that ended with her standing at her work table gazing out the front windows waiting for customers.

Across Greene Street was a two-story red brick building with businesses on the ground floor – a gift shop and a Mexican restaurant – and a hotel on the second floor. Behind the building Abby could see a large quaking aspen. She loved to watch the aspen leaves fluttering in the breeze. In the distance – across the Animas River – the slope of Kendall Mountain, green with spruce, pine and fir trees, soared to its peak of 13,000 feet.

She found herself thinking, *I love you.* She said it again, then again and again with the emphasis on a different word each time. She whispered out loud, "I'm in love with you. God, I love you. I love you so much that …"

A customer came in interrupting her reverie. "Hi," Abby said. "How're you doing?"

"Just fine. How bout you?"

"Couldn't be better," Abby replied with a big smile.

The customer had a toddler, a two-year-old boy who was shouting at the top of his lungs, "Mommy! Mommy! Trains! See the trains!"

Abby thought to herself, *I believe I prefer dogs to children in the Train Store. Dogs are better behaved.*

The child ran over to the display of toy trains, grabbed one out of a box, then he tore down the aisle to a toy train crossing light that was blinking red, yellow and green. The little boy stood on his tiptoes starring into the lights.

"Now, honey, you've got to put the train back. You've already got one of those," the boy's mother said.

"Sorry about that," she said to Abby. "He's just crazy about trains."

"Don't worry," Abby said. "That happens a lot. I often wonder why some little kids, boys especially, are so attracted to trains. What is it exactly that causes them to go ballistic when they come into the store?"

"It's just something about those big, powerful, choo-choos that sets them off."

"You'd think they'd be afraid of them, but they can't get enough of them. It might be because they're so loud. Little boys love anything noisy."

"Looks like we're going to have to buy that blinking light. How much is it?

"It's $29.95. I've got one in a box in the back. I'll be right back."

Abby wasn't always thrilled when small children came into the Train Store. It all depended on how much control their parents had over them. Sometimes the parents just let their kids run wild. The kids grabbed toys off the shelves and started playing with them on the floor, smashing into each other. When that happened, Abby told the parents if their kids were going to play with the toys they had to buy them. That brought the playing to a screeching halt. Other parents told their kids, "Hands in pockets," when they came into the store. That meant look but don't touch. Those were the families Abby preferred.

At least this woman bought something for her two-year-old.

Abby wrote "blinking light" on the list of the items she sold each day that she kept next to the cash register. Writing down the names of the prints, toys and posters she sold was her inventory system. It was primitive, but it worked for her. She didn't have to worry about a computer failing or losing files. If her pen ran out of ink there were plenty more in a box under the counter.

When the train arrived and customers started coming, in Abby got busy. Before she knew it she heard the four long whistles telling the riders to return to the train. Tom Walton hadn't come by for a visit.

After her customers left Abby had time to replenish her stock. Deflated but not defeated by Tom's failure to show up, she checked her inventory list and went about framing new prints and posters to replace the ones she had sold.

Then the phone rang.

"Silverton Train Store. This is Abby."

"Hi, this is Tom Walton. How are you?"

Abby couldn't believe it. Her voice leaped out of her throat. "I'm fine. How are you?"

"Just great. Listen, I wanted to stop by your store to see you today, but I was brakeman on the train, not engineer. The brakeman has to stay with the train when it's it town, so I couldn't escape. When I'm the engineer I can put the fireman in charge and leave the train for a few minutes."

"I understand," Abby said. "When will you be the engineer again?"

"Tomorrow. I'll be in to see you tomorrow."

"That's great. I'll be looking forward to seeing you."

"Okay. See you tomorrow."

"Thanks for calling." He had already hung up.

Abby felt a huge wave of relief wash over her. *He's thinking about me as much as I'm thinking about him,* she thought. *I can feel it. Wonder how he got my number? He must have picked up a Train Store business card the other day. I'll have to get his number so we can keep in touch.*

Diary entry for 5-8-14. "I know I've crossed a forbidden line, but I don't care. I wonder if others have known this feeling or if I'm the first person on Earth to possess this moment of truth. One thing is certain. I deserve it."

Chapter Nine

The next day a different engine powered the train –
number 482, a Baldwin built in Philadelphia in 1925 and
rebuilt in Durango in 1992. Four eighty-two was a K-36
class locomotive, more powerful than 473, but without
the tradition surrounding it.

Tom took the same joy piloting both locomotives. For
him they were living breathing things, dynamic metal
monsters alive to his touch. But that day his attention
was divided between the locomotive and the woman he
had met in Silverton a few days before. On the trip
north through the Animas River Canyon he thought of
her smile, her hair, the light in her eyes. He knew the
feelings he had for her were true.

Tom was quickly becoming everybody's favorite
D&SNGRR engineer. He was the guy who would
unfailingly smile and wave to everyone he passed in the
locomotive leaving Durango and alongside Highway

550 heading north and entering Silverton. He was the one who was happy to stand alongside passengers for photos when the train stopped and everyone got off. He didn't complain when he had to work as brakeman or fireman instead of being the engineer. He was just proud to be working on the railroad all the live long day.

He showed up at the Train Store right on time – one thirty in the afternoon. The sun was shining in a clear blue sky. Abby could not have been happier to see him. When he came in, she left the customer she was helping, dashed around the counter and threw her arms around him. He returned her hug enthusiastically.

"Hi, girl. How's business?"
He was wearing his work clothes – boots, bib overalls, blue shirt, blue bandana and engineer's hat.

"Couldn't be better. How are you?"

She experienced a rush of pure love. It felt like her

heart was about to soar right out of her chest.

"Had a good trip up today. As they say, when the train's full and the river's high, the boys are happy."

She looked up into his eyes. It seemed as if they were boring a hole down into the depths of her soul.

Returning to reality, she said, "I've got to help this lady."

The woman wanted to buy a Durango and Silverton train jigsaw puzzle.

"It's $15.95 plus tax. That's $17.61 total. Thanks."

Tom wandered around the store while Abby completed her sale.

Abby caught up with him in front of the pin display. "I wanted to ask how you got interested in trains?" she said.

"I grew up in a small town in Nebraska. Our house was next to a rail line that went out to a slaughter house at the edge of town. When I was six-years-old, me and my friend used to ride out of a ditch on stick horses with toy six shooters, wearing cowboy hats and bandanas covering our faces and hold up the trains going out to the slaughter house. They were diesels, not steam. The engineer would stop the train. He and the fireman would raise their hands, pretend like they were scared of us and let us climb on board. Then we would ride out to the slaughter house and back in the cab of the locomotive. I loved it. It wouldn't happen today with the railroads all automated and kids don't ride around on stick horses any more, but that's how trains came to be part of my life."

"I love that story."

"How'd you get into the train business?"

"Well, my husband and I have a friend named Herschel Scott who makes all the train art you see in the store and he wanted us to sell his prints and posters – so here I am."

"Your husband?"

Oops! Abby felt a chill run down her spine.
"I'm married. My husband has a store in Ouray. We're kind of separated."

That wasn't exactly true. They weren't really separated, but that's the way she felt. Abby didn't quite know how to continue the conversation, but Tom saved her. He didn't want to talk about her husband any more than she did.

Tom sniffed the air. "Are you cooking something in here?" he asked.

"You mean my perfume?" Abby grinned.

Tom laughed. "No. I love your perfume, but something smells like deep frying."

"That's the funnel cake shop next door. They're deep frying dough to make funnel cakes with all kinds of different toppings."

"Doesn't the aroma drive you crazy?"

"I don't notice it until someone mentions it. Then it's hard to resist."

Four long whistles reverberated from the corner of 12th and Blair where the train was waiting.

"That's my signal. I've got to get back to work."

"Please come back."

Without saying anything Tom turned his back and hurried out the door.

When the customers cleared out Abby went next door to tell Yvonne what had happened.

"I mentioned to Tom that I had a husband. I feel terrible."

"How did that subject come up?"

"I asked him how he got interested in trains and he had this cute story about holding up a train riding a stick horse when he was a kid. Then he asked me how I got in the train business and I blurted out it was through my husband and that was it. I was just being honest. I hadn't meant to say anything about Carl yet. I haven't thought how I'll approach the subject with Tom. It just slipped out."

"Did he say anything?"

"It was awkward. He changed the subject."

"Sometimes when people are told something they don't want to hear they kind of ignore it. It's an inconvenient truth. They just carry on as if nothing happened. The information gets stored in the back of their mind, but they don't act on it. That's what happened when someone told me my husband was cheating on me. I didn't want to believe it. I shut it out of my mind. I only believed it when I caught him and his floozy in the act in our bedroom – the bastard. Maybe that's what happened with Tom. He heard something he didn't want to know so it came in one ear and went out the other."

Abby gave Yvonne a hug. "I'm sorry about your ex, Yvonne. We'll see if Tom comes back. Can you do me a favor?"

"Sure. What is it?"

"You're a terrific photographer. Can you go over to 12th and Blair and take a picture of Tom in the engineer's seat when he arrives in town? Try to take it when he's looking at you and smiling."

"That's not hard. How do I know it's him?"

"Just yell, 'Hi, Tom.' If he looks at you and smiles it's him."

Yvonne could be sarcastic. "That's clever."

Diary entry for 5-9-14. "I'm terrified, but I feel wonderful at the same time. I now know how deep and how strong love can be. I just have to figure out a way to keep him in town for more than fifteen minutes at a time."

Chapter Ten

Silverton's weather came from the south and the southwest. Abby could always tell what the next day's weather would be by looking at what was happening in Los Angeles that morning. A Pacific Ocean storm had passed through L.A. on May 9 and sure enough, when she woke up on the 10th it was cold and raining in Silverton. Dense fog covered the town. Thunder came from somewhere high in the mountains. Not good train tourist weather, but the southwest was in the midst of a prolonged drought. The past winter had brought only half the normal amount of snow, so any moisture was welcome.

Abby went through her normal morning routine and put on her rain coat, but decided to drive her truck to work because she didn't want to get her feet wet walking. She went outside, pressed her key lock, climbed up the side steps and got in. Turning the engine on, she reveled in the powerful growl. After the truck warmed up for a few minutes she drove over to Greene Street.

Abby didn't want to take up a parking space in front of her store. She parked on the other side of Greene on the side street – 13th. The wind picked up and heavy raindrops began to fall as she walked to the shop, dodging puddles in the street.

Abby thought, *Spring rain – the first of the season. This would have been snow a couple of weeks ago. At least it'll wash the winter dirt off the street.*

Yvonne's door was closed. Abby unlocked the Train Store and went inside. There was no sun to warm the place. She turned on the three space heaters, with one of them blasting heat directly on her legs and the other two heating the back of the store. Even with the space heaters' warmth, she was glad she had worn her jeans and a knit sweater.

After a few chilly minutes Abby decided to turn on the pellet burning stove. It looked like an all-day rain and she wanted the store to be warm and welcoming for her customers. The pellets were made of pressed sawdust and each one was about the size of a large vitamin capsule. She poured pellets into the hopper in back of the stove, opened the front door and filled up the burn pot. Then she squeezed accelerant on the burn pot pellets, lit them and turned on the stove. An auger fed pellets from the hopper into the burn pot, where they were incinerated at a high temperature. A fan blew the heat into the room and before long the place had warmed up nicely.

Clouds covered the top of Kendall Mountain. Rain drummed on the metal roof of the Train Store building. Abby wondered if Tom Walton would make an appearance that day. She thought of a country song called *Under the Influence of Love,* sung by Buck Owens. That's how Abby felt. She couldn't help it. Tom Walton was all she thought about all the time. She was fixated on her engineer.

It turned out to be a quiet day. Most people didn't fancy walking around town getting soaked just to visit gift shops. They got off the train and stayed in the restaurants until it was time to leave.

A few customers came in the Train Store, dripping water on the floor.

"Can you tell us where's the best place in town to eat lunch?" a woman asked.

"All the restaurants in Silverton are one star," Abby said. The woman looked puzzled. "That's a joke. The most popular is Handlebars right around the corner from the Train Store. The most convenient is Natalia's. It's over on Blair Street across from where the train stops. You can have a long leisurely lunch there while you're waiting to reboard the train. Bent Elbow is across from Natalia's at the end of the block. Or you can eat pizza at the Avalanche, kitty-corner from the Bent Elbow."

"Thanks."

The people left without even looking around the store. Abby thought, *Don't let the door hit you in the butt on the way out.*

Will he come in today? she asked herself. She hoped so – even if it was a wet and messy day.

The skin at the edges of Abby's fingernails was cracked. Rubbing hand cream into her fingers, she was looking out the front window when she saw him walking quickly up the sidewalk across the street, past the Mexican restaurant, wearing a yellow raincoat and his engineer hat. Hunched over with his head down, but she couldn't miss him. He didn't look over at the Train Store. He crossed 13th street then she lost him. *Where's he going?* Abby asked herself. *Is it any of my business?* It looked like he was avoiding her on purpose. *Why didn't he at least wave? Was their connection all over and done with?*

Diary entry for 5-10-14: "Raining today. I saw Tom, but he didn't come in. It makes me feel bad. Rejection is the cancer of love, but I'll never give up on him. My love for him is so intense I'm going to use every means possible to make him love me. Everything is connected. Cause and effect is the universal rule. I believe forces deeper than I can comprehend have willed our union and nothing can break it."

Chapter Eleven

Sunday was Abby and Carl's day off when they closed
both stores and Carl came back to Silverton to spend
time with his wife. Usually, they went for a hike or
drove down to Durango to see a movie, but Abby hadn't
planned anything special for that Sunday. Waiting for
Carl, drinking her coffee, she was wearing sweat pants
and a T-shirt from a Silverton 4th of July 10K race. In
the background her 70's music station was playing *If
You Don't Know Me By Now* by Harold Melvin and the
Blue Notes.

For a man in his mid-50s Carl was holding up well.
He didn't think of himself as especially good-looking,
but he had even features, brown eyes. Fortunately, his
ears didn't stick out. He wasn't bald, ugly or
overweight. He was two inches shorter than Abby, but
he stayed fit and didn't smoke or drink. His hair was
graying and his hairline was receding, but he was
energetic and enjoyed being outdoors.

Carl showed up mid-morning. He was in a good mood and gave Abby a hug when he came into their house. He noticed her lack of enthusiasm in returning his greeting. Normally, they kissed when he came home on Sunday, but that day she turned her head away.

"How was your week?" he asked.

"Nothing great. How was yours?"

"Not bad. Had a couple of five hundred dollar days. Good for this time of year."

Abby didn't say anything.

"You're still wearing your sweat pants," Carl said. "Normally, you're dressed for our Sunday hike or the movies. Is something wrong?"

"Not really. Guess I'm just tired."

Carl opened the refrigerator and helped himself to an apple. Little things Carl did were starting to aggravate Abby. She hated the crunching noise he made when he ate the fruit.

"Listen, on my drive over Red Mountain I was thinking about our plans for this winter. We always take a couple of months off in January and February when there's fewer tourists. I've heard of a great place in Mexico called San Carlos on the Gulf of California where a couple of Silverton people have bought property. What do you think of going down there, renting a place and maybe going whale watching or we could rent a sailboat? You've always wanted to go sailing."

"No thanks." Watching Tom walk by the store without coming in had put Abby in a bad mood. "Can you close your mouth when you're eating that apple? You're drowning out the music."

"Really? Sorry." Carl tossed his half eaten apple in the trash.

"Is something the matter?" he asked. "You're not interested in Mexico? I thought you'd jump at the chance to go. It's warm all winter down there. We always talk about where we're going to spend the winter. "

"I had a tough day yesterday at the store. It rained and business was bad."

"Okay. Whatever. We don't need to talk about this right now."

"I've got some stuff to do in the shop. I'll see you later."

Abby had a work shop in the garage in back of the house where she cut mats and printed posters.

She wound up spending all day in her shop. Carl went out to his favorite hiking trail in Cunningham Gulch and didn't return until late afternoon.

When he got back, Carl stuck his head in the shop. "Hey, you want to go out for dinner? Handlebars? Shouldn't be too crowded. Not that many tourists on a Sunday night."

"No thanks. I'm not hungry. You can go if you want."

Carl hated dining out alone. He felt stupid sitting at a table for one with no one to talk to while he waited for his food. He went back to the house and put a frozen two-person lasagna in the microwave. When it was ready he ate half.

When Abby came in from her shop Carl said, "I left some lasagna for you." But she didn't acknowledge him. Instead, she went straight to the bedroom and closed the door. When Carl tried to open the bedroom door, he found it locked.

"Hey, Abby. You locked the door. What for? Open up. I want to go to bed."

But Abby didn't open the door. She was in the bathroom standing naked under the shower, facing the spray, eyes closed, her hands on her breasts, fantasizing about Tom Walton. *How it would feel to be alone with him. What she would say to him. What they would do when they were together.*

Carl was listening. He could hear the shower from the living room. When Abby turned it off, he knocked on the door and yelled, "Come on Abby! This is bullshit! Let me in!"

Abby ignored him. She toweled off, blow dried her hair and crawled between the sheets naked. She fell asleep quickly and dreamed deeply.

In Abby's dream a hummingbird returned repeatedly to a flower to drink in its aroma, to inhale its beauty. When she woke up she remembered her dream and thought she must be the hummingbird because she was attracted irresistibly to Tom Walton.

That night Carl slept alone on the day bed in the sun room. Normally on Monday mornings Abby fixed breakfast for him, but that morning she stayed in the bedroom waiting for Carl to leave.

He stood at the bedroom door.

"I've got to go back to Ouray. I don't know what's going on with you. Whatever's wrong, we need to talk about it."

Chapter Twelve

Conflicting emotions battered Carl on his drive to Ouray over Red Mountain Pass – anger, hurt, feelings of rejection. He didn't like being locked out of his bedroom and he didn't like not having breakfast before he left Silverton. All of a sudden Abby was mad at him. He felt like he had been ambushed.

Carl thought back over the past few months, wondering what could have set her off. He couldn't remember any serious arguments or disagreements. He thought they got along well. They only saw each other once a week on Sunday, at least in the summer. He missed her during the week and was always happy to see her when they got back together and she reciprocated – or at least he thought she did. The only serious disagreement he recalled them having was when she wanted to buy her truck. But that was two years ago. Carl shook his head, perplexed. He thought, *You just never know when resentments will surface.*

Carl drove a ten-year-old Subaru. He liked the way it handled driving to Ouray on Highway 550 with all the curves and switchbacks. He hated making car payments and didn't need to buy a new car every two or three years like a lot of people did. He recalled arguing with Abby about her decision to buy the big pickup truck. Her truck cost twice as much as his Subaru and he had almost as much room in the back of his car as she did in the bed of her truck. He thought she was crazy to spend so much money on a vehicle she didn't use very much, but he stopped objecting to the truck once she bought it. He wanted to move on. Carl knew when Abby made up her mind about something there was no turning back. She was stubborn.

Carl knew all about stubborn people. His dad was stubborn. As a young man Mats Lindgren had emigrated from Sweden, a place called Almhult, where his family had a farm. He told them he didn't want to be a farmer and found his way to Salinas, California, where he worked as a truck mechanic and married Carl's mother, Rachel. Mats wanted Carl to follow in his footsteps and be a truck mechanic. Carl worked in Mats' garage when he was a teenager, but Mats was a perfectionist. Nothing Carl did, no repair he made, was ever good enough for his dad. Carl remembered Mats berating him, telling him he was careless with his tools, he didn't clean up after a job or he wasn't working hard enough. When he graduated from high school, Carl left home and moved down the road to Fresno.

He married Shelly, his high school sweetheart, and they had a couple of kids. He supported his young family and put himself through business school in Fresno by working as a mechanic in a garage. He talked to his mother on the phone and he brought his family home for Christmas, but he never lived in Salinas again. His parents, especially Mats, were unhappy with him when he and his first wife divorced. They were afraid they would lose contact with their grandchildren, but Shelly moved back to Salinas, so they were able to see the kids.

After moving to Fresno Carl stayed in touch with his childhood friend, Herschel Scott. He admired Scotty's artistic talent and thought he could make a good business out of selling Scotty's art work. The two of them got together and opened a store in Leavenworth, Washington, where Carl met Abby.

Carl realized he had spent his entire adult life avoiding his father. Now Abby's negative attitude was beginning to remind Carl of Mats, but he didn't want to go through another divorce. The first one had been too painful. He decided to get to the bottom of whatever Abby's problem was and to do everything he could to save their marriage.

Midmorning, Carl arrived at Wheels, Wings and Nautical Things, his store on Main Street in Ouray. He parked around the corner, opened up, and turned on the lights. Then he put up a "Welcome" flag outside the door, hung up some plant holders and stuck a couple of lawn flamingoes in a pot on the sidewalk.

Inside, the shop was divided into three areas for items related to cars and trucks, boats and airplanes. Carl sold playing cards and games like cribbage and Mexican Hat as well as the same posters of national parks created by Herschel Scott that Abby sold at her store. His walls were full of metal signs advertising popular motorcycles of the 1950s and 60s like BSA and Norton and gasoline companies like Phillips 66 that were no longer in business. Carl's business model appealed to nostalgia, his customers' childhood memories of classic vehicles and iconic businesses that no longer existed. In Carl's imagination, his store offered all the good things our current culture has lost.

Chapter Thirteen

After Carl left for Ouray, Abby stood in front of her bathroom mirror brushing her hair, thinking of Tom — *What should I wear to work that he would like?* Looking in her closet, she wondered what colors he preferred. Should she change her perfume? She decided not to wear a bra. She put on her jeans and a short-sleeved, blue blouse with red piping around the arms and neck.

She found Yvonne as usual sitting in the sun outside My Things.

"Hi dear," Yvonne greeted Abby. "You look nice today. That's a pretty blouse. It looks familiar. Dressing for someone special?"

"Thank you, Yvonne. It should. I bought the blouse from you. And yes, it's for someone special. I think about him every day. When he comes in the store I get a hot flash. It's like an involuntary reaction to seeing him."

"Sort of like when you wash your hands you have to pee?"

"Haha. Very funny, but yes, I guess it's kind of like that. I dreamed about him last night and he was my first thought when I woke up this morning. I talk to myself about him. Even when I'm talking to you or a customer I'm still thinking about him."

"Sounds like this has gone beyond the schoolgirl crush stage."

"I can't believe it's happening. I've only spoken to him twice for a few minutes each time. But here I am, head over heels in love."

"What about Carl?"

"I locked him out of our bedroom last night. He had

to sleep in the sun room."

"I'm sure he was thrilled. Why'd you do that?"

"I just didn't want to be around him. He interfered with my fantasizing about Tom."

"Are you going to tell Carl about Tom?"

"I guess I'll have to at some point, but right now there's really nothing to tell. I don't know if Tom feels the same way about me as I feel about him. It's like I'm a love addict, but I'm in the closet until Tom lets me out."

"That's a novel way of putting it."

"Love is making me creative."

"Do you see a future for you and Carl?"

"Ya. Boring."

"What would your future with Tom look like?"

"I don't know. I just want to be with him. We'll figure it out. Time to open up. Let me go. It's a sunny day. Maybe he'll come in."

Chapter Fourteen

With the train in town, the sidewalks filled with
crowds of people from all over the U.S. and around the
world. Lines formed outside restaurants. Tourists were
everywhere − taking pictures of store fronts with their
phone cameras; walking backwards down Greene Street
shooting videos; gawking at the mountain scenery,
oblivious of cars, motorcycles and ATVs.

Business was booming. Abby stayed busy through the
morning and past lunch. She was helping a customer
and didn't notice Tom when he entered the store. When
she finished at the cash register, she looked up and there
he was.

"Oh, hi!" Abby blushed. "Sorry. I didn't see you
come in. I was busy."

"That's all right. You look great in that blouse. Blue
is my favorite color."

She reveled in his admiration. Without the confinement of a bra, Abby's nipples strained against her blouse as if they were reaching out to him.

"What engine did you drive today?"

"Good old 473. Hey, listen. I've got something for you. Let's go over to that mirror you have on the wall over there."

Abby sold engineer and conductor hats as well as baseball-style caps with railroad logo patches sewn on them. The mirror was placed on the wall above the hat section of the store so customers could see how they looked wearing one.

Abby was excited. Her heart was pounding. This was unexpected. *What's he got?* She faced him in front of the mirror.

"Turn around."

She did as she was told. Tom took a small box from his pocket. Inside the box, nestled in cotton, was a delicate sterling silver necklace with a steam locomotive pendant. He took the necklace out of the box. With one end of the necklace in each hand, he rested the pendant on her chest and brought his hands around to the back of her neck.

Abby could see the necklace in the mirror.

"Oh, Tom. Thank you. It's what I've always wanted."

She reached back and held up her hair.

He opened the clasp with his finger nail.

"I'm not very good at this," he mumbled as he struggled to fasten the clasp of the necklace chain.

She moved a step back so her backside pressed against

the front of his overalls and she could feel him.

"Maybe the chain is too small," he said.

"You're doing just fine," she murmured.

The sight of Abby's bare neck and being so close to her produced a stirring in Tom's overalls. His voice became husky.

"There. I've got it." His lips brushed her neck under her ear. "How do you like it?"

Looking in the mirror, Abby exclaimed, "Oh, Tom. It's gorgeous. I love it!"

She turned around to face him. "I'm never taking it off."

"Even in the shower?"

"Especially in the shower." Abby looked steadily into Tom's eyes. His eyes were so deep she saw herself not so much reflected in them as lost in them – and she was powerless to look away.

Tom was a couple of inches taller than Abby. She liked looking up at him. She reached up and touched his cheek. He took her hand in his and pressed her palm to his lips. The warmth of his body came into hers and spread wherever it wanted to go. She stood on her toes, lifted her head and kissed him hungrily.

She felt the heat from his face as he reddened and kissed her back passionately.

Desire overwhelmed Abby for an instant. A wetness spread between her legs.

Several ladies in the store looked on, grinning their approval.

"Look what he gave me!" she gushed, showing them

her new necklace.

"It's beautiful," one of the women said.

"Where did you buy it?" Abby asked.

"The Baker Park Jewelry Store across the street in the next block. I bought it yesterday."

"It was raining yesterday."

"Yes, it was. The rain was my excuse for not coming in the store. I bought your necklace instead."

That explained Tom's sneaking up the other side of Greene Street in the rain. Abby decided not to tell Tom she had seen him the day before. She didn't want him to think she was spying on him.

"When's your birthday?" Abby asked.

"Not until October. I'll be fifty. Kind of scary. When's yours?"

"It's today!" Abby grinned. "Just kidding. It's in January, but it feels like my birthday's today and this necklace is the best present I've ever gotten. I forget how old I am."

Just then four long whistles sounded.
"Gotta get back," he said.

"I wish you could stay." She hugged him tightly, crushing her breasts against his chest.

"I do too." He returned her hug. "Let's work something out."

"Call me. Please."

Tom was out of breath when he got back to the train. Seated on his perch in the cab of engine 473, he exclaimed to his fireman, Chase, "Heckuva day, isn't it?" The day seemed pretty ordinary to Chase, but he didn't say anything. Tom Walton felt exuberant.

"Did you check those air brakes?" Tom asked Chase.

"Yessir. We're good to go."
"What about the cab brakes?"

"Yessir. We're leaning foward."

"It's time to head back down the canyon."

Tom put extra vigor into the two long whistles signaling the train was about to start its downhill journey to Durango.

Diary entry for 5-12-14: "There is no difficulty that enough love will not conquer; no disease that enough love will not cure; no door that enough love will not open; no sin that enough love will not redeem. This I

117

believe: if I can love Tom Walton enough I will be the happiest and most successful woman on the face of this earth."

Chapter Fifteen

After closing the Train Store, Abby went next door. She wanted to show Yvonne her new necklace.

"Look what Tom gave me."

"It's a steam locomotive," Yvonne said, holding the pendant. "On a fine silver chain. Very pretty. And appropriate. Your man is thinking about you. That's important. Where'd he get it?"

"The Baker Park Jewelry Store in the next block across the street."

"They have some nice things. Did you ask how much he paid for it?"

"Yvonne! That's not nice."
The two women laughed.

Yvonne put up the "Closed" sign in her shop window. Turning to her friend, she said, "It's time for a serious discussion about your marriage. What's your relationship with Carl? Are you lovers? Best friends?"

"Lovers? God, no! There's no passion in our relationship. I don't think there ever was. Sex was a duty, not a pleasure. Best friends? Besties? No. You're my best friend, Yvonne. Carl and I are business partners. That's it. I haven't known you for more than a couple of years, but I feel much closer to you than I do to Carl and I've known him for almost twenty years. Isn't that odd?"

"Do you and Carl share a bed?"

"Yes, we sleep in the same bed, but nothing happens. There's no intimacy. We don't have sex very often. It's like sleeping with my brother."

"Do you like Carl?"

"Well, yes. I guess so."

"That's not a very encouraging answer."

"It's like liking something on Facebook. There's not a lot of energy behind it."

"That's cruel, Abby."

"I know. I shouldn't be talking about him like this. We've shared a lot of dreams, a lot of struggles, a lot of history. I'm just bored."

"How old is Carl?"

"He's fifty-four."

"What about Tom"

"He's closer to my age. He'll be fifty on his next birthday in October."

"Four years difference between Carl and Tom. Not a big deal."

"Tom just seems more my generation than Carl is. Carl's kind of old school."

"Silverton is an old school kind of place. So is your Train Store. You celebrate lots of railroads that no longer exist."

"That's true. How did we get started on this?"

"Talking about age differences. What's Carl like to do?"

"He's pretty wrapped up in his business. He likes to hike and he watches a lot of sports on TV."

"Sounds like a typical American guy."

"Ya. I guess so."

While Abby was talking to Yvonne, she fingered the train pendant of her new necklace. When she realized what she was doing she said, "Do you know what Carl gave me for my birthday?"

"No. What?"

"A gift certificate to his store! Can you believe that?"

"How much?"

"What was the gift certificate worth? Fifty dollars! Whoopeedoo!"

"At least it wasn't twenty. As they say, it's the thought that counts. Did you cash it in?"

"I sure did! I took fifty dollars' worth of stuff from his store, marked it up and sold it in my store. I made a tidy profit."

"I always knew you're a smart business lady."

"Carl never gave me anything I couldn't resist holding onto. Like this pendant Tom gave me. That tells you something."

"He probably gave you lots of stuff you don't think about."

"You know who I feel like?"

"No, who?"

"Francesca in *Bridges of Madison County*. Did you read it?"

"I tried, but it was too mushy. I couldn't finish it. But I saw the movie. Meryl Streep as Francesca and Clint Eastwood as the photographer guy. What was his name?"

"Robert Kincaid."

"Yes. Great movie. I loved it. God, he was hot."

"Meryl and Clint sleep together in the film. I fantasize about sleeping with Tom."

"Have you ever cheated on Carl?"

"No, I haven't. At least not yet."
"Do you think Carl has someone in Ouray?"

"I never thought of that. It hasn't occurred to me. I don't care if he does. There's just something missing in our relationship. It's a big something."

"Yes, it's called Carl. He's never here. Do you think if he was here you'd be attracted to Tom?"

"Yes, I do. Definitely."

"Are you sure you're not being selfish? Self-centered? Maybe Carl has needs that aren't being met by you. What would you feel like if he started an affair with another woman?"

"I never thought of that. Our needs are different. All he cares about is the business − making money. I don't think he has emotional needs. As long as he can pay our bills he's satisfied."

"Do you want to divorce Carl?"

"That's a big question. No. I don't know. Maybe. I can't give you a yes or no answer right this second. As the song says, 'There's nothing cold as ashes after the fire has gone,' but I'm not there yet. I guess it depends on what happens with Tom, but I will tell you that with Tom Walton I feel like I've won the Colorado Lottery."

Diary entry for 5-15-14: This is what it's like to have an open heart, to believe the force of love can change your life."

Chapter Sixteen

Overnight the temperature had dipped below 32 degrees. The next morning a layer of wood smoke hung over Silverton. Abby wore a quilted coat on her walk to work. She sat down next to Yvonne on the bench in front of My Things.

"Chilly day," Yvonne said. She was wearing a wool coat that reached down to her ankles.

Abby offered her friend some of the snack she brought to work. "Hungry?"

"What's that?"

"Trail mix – M & M's, raisins, peanuts. Carl makes it for me."

"That's nice of him. No thanks. Stuff like that gets in my teeth and gives me cavities. I can't afford to go to the dentist."

Abby put the trail mix back in her lunch bag. "You know what?"

"No. What?"

"I have a guilty secret."

"You mean besides your crush on your train engineer?"

"Yes. But maybe it's related. You remember yesterday when I told you I felt like I'd won the Colorado Lottery with Tom?"

"Yes."

"Well, I've been playing the lottery, buying tickets every week."

"And you feel guilty about it?"

"Yes. Kind of. You know what I mean. It's gambling. Carl says when I play the lottery I'm just throwing money away."

"Why are you gambling on the lottery?"

"Seeing if I win anything gives me something to look forward to, but that was before I met Tom. Now I look forward to seeing him. I guess I like to fantasize about what I'll do when I win a hundred million dollars."

"So what's your fantasy?"

"I'm going to buy a big black Cadillac SUV with Wi-fi if they have it."

"I'm sure they must. Caddies have got to have Wi-fi if Chevies do."

"You think so?"

"I'm positive. Cadillacs are old school. Why don't you get some kind of electric car like a Tesla? Or a Jaguar."

"Are Jaguars electric?"

"I don't know. You'll have all this money to spend. You can buy one of each. Jaguars are cool."

"The Caddie goes with my truck. Both GM."

"Okay. Whatever. What else?"

"What else what?"

"What else are you going to do with your hundred million dollars?"

"Maybe I'll take you out to lunch."

"Thanks a lot. Have you ever won anything?"

"Four dollars a couple of times for matching the Powerball number. The big games are Powerball and Mega Millions. You know what?"

Yvonne thought Abby's flirtation with Tom Walton is bringing out the kid in her. "No. What?"

"I'm having second thoughts about winning big. Sometimes nobody wins Powerball and Mega Millions for months and the jackpots build up to half a billion dollars. That's just way too much money. I'd be overwhelmed by that much money. I think it would make me unhappy."

"You could give me half."
"That's a thought."

"So half a billion dollars makes you unhappy − even though you haven't won it yet. How much do you want to win?"

"Around five million would be nice. Five million is doable. I want to win one of the smaller games like Lotto or Lucky for Life. You get $1000 a day forever when you win Lucky for Life."

"I'll tell whoever's in charge at lottery headquarters."

"Thanks. Meanwhile I've got Tom."

"That's true. Do you play special lucky numbers?"

"No. I just take what the machine gives me."

"Since you've got this connection with the train and Tom Walton maybe you should play D and S engine numbers – 473, 482."

Abby lit up with a big smile. "That's a great idea, Yvonne. Why didn't I think of it?"

Diary entry for 5-16-14: "I used to think my dream

man would be a sophisticated San Franciscan, a diplomat, an artist, maybe a baseball player. Instead, he turned out to be a steam train engineer from Nebraska. Who knew?"

Chapter Seventeen

The next time Tom stopped by the Train Store, Abby had a present for him. There were only a few customers in the store. After exchanging hugs Abby said, "Close your eyes."

"What for?"

"I've got something for you."

"All right. If you insist."

Abby brought out a black gift box.

"Hold out your hand."

Tom did as he was told.

Abby placed the box on his palm.
"Open your eyes."

He looked at her with his cobalt-blue eyes. He was drawn to this woman like no other in his life.

Abby blushed. It was all about just the two of them together.

"You can open the box."

Smiling, Tom opened the box. Inside, nestled in a bed of cotton, was a silver bracelet with designs etched on it.

"This is a handsome gift. Thank you so much."

Tom enveloped Abby in his arms, then looked closer at the bracelet. "Where'd you get it?"

"At the Indian jewelry store on the corner. It's sterling silver. Feel how heavy it is."

"What do these decorations mean? They're engraved on the bracelet."

"It's a Hopi design alternating three ocean waves with three mountain tops across the bracelet. Look inside."

Inscribed on the inside was "To Tom from Abby with love, 5/20/14."

"I don't know what to say. I'm touched. No one has ever given me anything like this."

"Put it on."

Tom struggled to put the bracelet on his wrist. "It's kind of small."

Abby took his hand in hers and shook it. "Relax. Don't go all tense on me. Make your wrist go limp."

The bracelet slipped easily from the side onto Tom's wrist. "Do I have to start talking with a lisp?"

"Don't be silly. Lots of men wear bracelets. It's sexy."

"If you say so. Thank you."

He wrapped her in his arms and gave her a big hug, lifting her off the floor and whispering in her ear, "I love it. I'll never take it off."

After the train pulled out and the store was empty, Abby stood at her work table absent-mindedly framing mini-posters to replace the ones she had sold. She was day-dreaming. She imagined dancing with Tom, the two of them together traveling far away on a ship, standing on a tropical beach, their arms entwined.

What was it about Tom that attracted her? She thought he was brave to drive the train and even daring – but there was a tenderness about him and she knew he was capable of devotion since he kept coming to visit her. That was important. And there was an "otherness" about Tom that Abby didn't understand, but she found it irresistible.

Diary entry for 5-20-14: "Before I met Tom my heart was an ice cube. I felt cold, like a robot. Now when I'm in his arms I'm alive. My heart is full. It feels superheated, on the verge of melting. I'm becoming a whole woman."

Chapter Eighteen

Standing at her work table the next day, Abby thought that with a new boyfriend, the height of tourist season fast approaching and business picking up, she was happy with her life. Just before noon the sound of the train whistle echoed off the sides of the mountains surrounding Silverton. Each engineer gave the whistle his own special twist, making the sound a little different every day. Abby thought she could pick out Tom's whistle from the others. Little did she know that sound would soon be missing from Silverton for days stretching into weeks.

Two trains arrived that day. Tourists filled the restaurants. After lunch they strolled down Greene Street entering the businesses, the women shopping, the men restless, eager to return to the trains. Abby kept busy, making sales and talking to people.

One of her customers asked, "What's it like here during the winter?"

"It gets real quiet. We're busy in the summer with the train bringing tourists up here, but most people don't want to drive over two 11,000-foot-high passes covered with snow in the winter. That's unless they're winter recreation types – skiers or snowmobilers. We get them in town, but they aren't interested in train stuff. So for the six months of winter we're a quiet retreat tucked away in the wilderness. Where do you live?"

"Phoenix. It's hot now, but nice in the winter."

"I don't think I could put up with 120 degrees in the summer."

"You get used to it. Just go from your air-conditioned house to your air-conditioned car to your air-conditioned office or mall."

"I don't think there's a single air conditioner in Silverton. We're got natural air conditioning."

"It never snows in Phoenix. Maybe I'll come up here in the winter. See what it's like."

"I think it's prettier in the winter. And there's far fewer people."

Around one o'clock a young man dressed like a D&S employee came into the Train Store. Abby thought she recognized him, but she wasn't sure.

"Hi. I'm Chase, Tom Walton's fireman. He asked me to tell you he won't be in today. Something's happened with the train."

Abby's heart jumped. Her hand went to her mouth. "He's okay, isn't he?"

"Yes. The passengers and crew are fine. It's a problem down the line. I have to get back."

As Chase left the store, Abby wanted to say, Tell him I

love him, but she caught herself and called out, "Tell him we're thinking about him."

One of Abby's lady customers overheard the exchange between Abby and Chase.

"I was riding in the open observation car of the second train," the woman said. "After we left Durango everything was fine. Everybody was lined up along the outside wall of the car taking pictures. We crossed the highway and climbed a hill for a ways. I was looking back and all of a sudden I saw what looked like a smoke explosion along the tracks. We went around a curve and I couldn't see the tracks behind us anymore, but there appeared to be a cloud of smoke rising behind us. At the time I wondered if the train had started a fire."

"Fires along the tracks are a problem," Abby said. "Especially when we're under the drought conditions we have now. It's been dry. We had a lot less snow than normal this past winter. The last rain was almost two weeks ago. Usually, there's a rail car — they call it a pop car — fitted with some fire-fighting equipment that follows the train and puts out small fires that start from sparks coming out of the stack. Up until now, that's always worked. And there's a fire arrester around the top of the stack that cuts down on the amount of sparks flying out, but you never know. I hope everything's all right."

"I do too. I don't want to be stuck here overnight if the train's delayed."

Abby wanted to close the door and go over to 12th and Blair to see what was happening, but people were milling around in the store, making it hard for her to leave. Soon she saw two D&S buses coming up Greene Street. They turned on 13th and headed over to Blair. The buses were followed by a convoy of four Durango school buses and two D&S vans. Abby knew what that meant. The passengers from the two trains were not riding back to Durango in cars pulled by steam engines.

Instead, they would be traveling south on buses. The vans were for the train crews. A major problem must have developed for that to happen.

Eventually, all the customers cleared out of the store and Abby was able to turn the "Open" sign around to "Closed". She locked the door and hurried down Greene to the corner just in time to see a van leaving. Tom Walton was looking out the window of the van in Abby's direction. He saw her and waved. She sank down on her haunches without waving back, unable to move as she watched the van leaving town.

Abby remained squatting in the dusty street for a few minutes, then rose to her feet and returned to the Train Store. She went in, left the "Closed" sign where it was, sat down on her stool behind the counter and wept. Bitterly. On the radio Dwight Yoakam was singing *A Thousand Miles From Nowhere*. That's how Abby felt. Her heart was aching and there were tear stains on her hands.

That afternoon Abby didn't write in her diary. She didn't know how to put into words what she was feeling.

Chapter Nineteen

When she finally pulled herself together, Abby walked over to Blair Street. Two full trains were parked there on parallel rail lines on 12th – engines, tenders, passenger cars, observation cars, food and bar cars – all locked and quiet. Abandoned. That's how Abby felt.

She needed to talk to someone, so she went back to Greene Street to see if Yvonne was still in her store. She was tallying the day's receipts when Abby walked in.

"Did you hear anything about a fire?" Abby asked.

"The sheriff stopped by and told me the second train started a brush fire along the tracks about ten miles north of Durango. The entire La Plata County Fire Department has been called out. The train can't go back to Durango and the highway is closed. There's too much smoke and they're afraid the train will catch on fire if it gets showered with sparks from the fire. They loaded all the passengers into buses and took them back to Durango the long way around through Ridgway, then down through Dolores and Mancos. You look terrible. Have you been crying?"

"Yes. I went over to 12th and Blair and saw Tom just as he was leaving town in a train van. He waved. It was like that was it and we'd never see each other again."

"It all sounds really serious. We'll just have to wait and see. By the way, this morning I went over and took a picture of Tom when he pulled in. Your trick worked great. I shouted 'Hi, Tom,' he leaned out of his engine window, smiled and I shot the picture. He's a nice-looking man. Cheer up. I'm sure he'll be back. Or at least he'll call."

"I'm hoping he does. There's so much I want to say to him. Tell me how much it costs to develop the picture so I can pay for it."

"I'll go to Walgreens and have it enlarged. After the highway opens up. Shouldn't be long."

Chapter Twenty

But it was. The brush fire along the tracks turned into the Hermosa Cliffs Fire, a major wildfire that engulfed Highway 550 for several miles, then blew westward consuming thousands of acres in the San Juan National Forest. In addition to the La Plata County Fire Department, U.S. Forest Service Hotshot fire-fighting teams came in from Idaho, Montana, Wyoming, Arizona and throughout Colorado to fight the blaze.

With the highway closed and the train not operating, just as the tourist season was shifting into high gear, business in Silverton slowed to a trickle. All the stores, restaurants and motels remained open for the time being, but there were few customers. The fire burned ten miles north of Durango and thirty miles to the south and west of Silverton. Neither town was in any physical danger, but economic damage was being done and smoke from the fire covered both towns and the surrounding mountains.

Abby had written out the daily train schedule on a piece of paper and taped it to a metal ceiling support next to her work desk. When the trains stopped coming to town, she took her king-size black magic marker and wrote CANCELLED in capital letters across the schedule. That's what she felt had happened to her life. It had been CANCELLED.

A few days after the fire started, Abby sat down next to Yvonne.

"You know, I think I miss the sound of the train whistle most of all. More than the customers, more than the business. It's such a distinctive sound. I could tell when Tom was pulling the whistle cord."

"I know what you mean. It's called the train whistle blues." Yvonne started coughing.

"That was a Jimmie Rodgers song back in the day," Abby said, brightening. "Remember the singing brakeman? This smoke is downright unhealthy. My eyes are watering."

"It's worst in the morning. I can feel it in my throat and my nose. Everything is in a haze. You can't see the Grenadier peaks down through the Animas River Valley gap. That's my favorite view. At least the wind picks up in the afternoon and blows most of the smoke way. I wonder how Ouray is doing. Have you spoken to Carl?"

"Before the fire I was going to call and tell him not to come on Sunday. My excuse was I was dealing with some issues and needed to be by myself. But I've been so depressed by this whole thing that I need someone to be around after work – even Carl – so I called and asked if he was coming. He said yes, but made me promise not to lock him out of the bedroom."

"This will give the two of you a chance to talk about your marriage. If you're ready."

"That's a talk I'm dreading. He has no idea about

Tom. He did say that business in Ouray has slowed down too. Apparently CDOT, the Colorado highway department, put up a sign in Ridgway that the highway from Silverton to Durango is closed and people should turn right on Highway 62 and go down through Dolores and Mancos if they want to get to Durango. That means tourists aren't traveling to Ouray and they sure aren't coming to Silveron."

"Jeez. This is awful. My business is down 50%. Some of the businesses on Blair Street are down 80%. At least we're still getting hikers and ATV people."

Chapter Twenty-One

But the hikers and ATV people didn't last. The next day, citing safety concerns, the Forest Service closed the San Juan National Forest to all hikers and motor vehicles. That meant mostly jeeps and All Terrain Vehicles (ATVs). Eighty-six percent of San Juan County is owned by the federal government and managed by the U.S. Forest Service and the Bureau of Land Management (BLM).

The San Juan National Forest covered the dirt roads and mountains west of Silverton. The Weminuche Wilderness, managed by the Forest Service, lay to the south. BLM land was to the north of town. The BLM area was still open to hikers and ATVs, but most tourists didn't know the difference between the Forest Service and the BLM. They just knew there was a dangerous fire near Silverton so they cancelled their plans to come to southwest Colorado and went elsewhere.

As the month of June progressed, Silverton's economy dried up completely. Businesses, especially restaurants, began to close. Employees were laid off and left town to look for work someplace else. One thousand fire-fighting personnel were deployed to fight the Hermosa Cliffs Fire. Over three hundred homes and businesses were evacuated, including Purgatory Resort. Air tankers and helicopters dropped fire-retardant slurry on the flames. Traffic on Highway 550 stopped from both the north and the south.

That Sunday Carl arrived at the house around ten. His Subaru had been the only vehicle on the highway coming over Red Mountain Pass. Normally − especially in June − there would be a fair amount of traffic traveling through the San Juan Mountains.

He found Abby sitting in the kitchen, looking out the window at the mountains, drinking coffee and listening to the radio. Willie Nelson was singing *Blue Eyes Crying in the Rain* on satellite radio.

They exchanged greetings, but not hugs.

"Get yourself some coffee," Abby said without much enthusiasm.

When he sat down with his cup, Carl said, "I saw pictures of the fire on NBC News last night. It's beautiful and awful."

"Fearful and wonderful, somebody called it. People are putting 'Thank You, Firefighters' signs on their businesses."

"Sounds like the right thing to do. Are you going to put one up?"

"I haven't decided yet. Do you think they'll ever put it out?"

"The only think that will put this fire out is snow this winter."

"That's encouraging."

Carl noticed the steam locomotive necklace Abby was wearing. She had thought of taking it off before he got there, but had forgotten.

"Where'd you get the necklace?"

Abby's face turned red. She hadn't prepared herself for this moment. A thought flashed through her mind. *Trust is what defines a relationship.* Looking Carl in the eye, she had to think quickly. I've got two choices: tell him the truth and watch our marriage dissolve in front of me or lie and save our marriage – at least for the time being.

Long pause. Inhale. The picture of Tom Walton waving as he left town in the van flickered before Abby's eyes. It had been four days and he hadn't called. She wasn't sure of him anymore. She wasn't ready to make the big decision. So she lied.

"I saw it at the Baker Park Jewelry Store and had to have it for myself." Exhale. Abby realized she had never lied to Carl before. "Do you like it?"

"Yes. It's pretty and appropriate for you and the store. Do you want to talk about anything?"

"You mean why I locked you out of the bedroom last Sunday?"

"That's a good place to start."

"I've just been real unhappy recently. I can't put my finger on exactly what my problem is."

"Was it something I did or said?"

"No. Not really."

"But you took it out on me. That wasn't fair."

"I'm sorry, Carl. I think it's running the business for fourteen years. I'm getting bored with it. And now the train has shut down. Maybe I need a change."

Carl thought that perhaps Abby's moodiness was due to early onset menopause, but he didn't want to come right out and say it. She was still only in her early 40's.

"You know as well as I do that we need the income from two businesses in order to make ends meet – especially when you insist on buying an expensive truck instead of a cheaper automobile."

"Let's not get started on that again."

"Okay. Do you want to switch businesses? I can take over the Train Store while you run Wheels Wings and Nautical Things."

Abby hadn't thought of that, but it was a non-starter. Being in Ouray would take her away from Tom.

"That's an interesting suggestion. Let me think about it."

"You want to go for a hike?"

"We can't hike in the national forest, but I guess you know that. BLM land is still open. Sure. Why not?"

"Any place you want to go?"

"No. You decide while I get dressed."

Carl filled their water bottles and put some energy bars in his pockets. They drove out County Road 2, then turned right into Cunningham Gulch. At the end of the gulch they drove through Cunningham Creek, parked at the trail head and hiked the trail up to the Highland Mary Lakes and back. Normally, they would have encountered other hikers on the trail, but Carl and Abby were all alone that day.

When they returned to the car, Abby said, "You know, I feel a lot better. Being out in the wilderness like this makes me happy. Maybe that's what I've been missing." She gave Carl a hug. "Thanks for the hike."

Driving back to Silverton, Carl asked, "You want to go out for dinner?"

"All right. Feel like pizza? How bout the Avalanche?"

"Sounds great." Carl thought, It looks like she's recovering from her funk. We'll see.

They shared a pizza and a pitcher of beer at the Avalanche Cafe. When they returned home Carl said, "Mind if I take a shower first? I feel kind of grungy."

"That's fine with me."

By the time Abby had her turn to take a shower Carl

was fast asleep. She crept into bed and was careful not to wake him. On Monday morning, Carl went back to Ouray after Abby fixed him breakfast.   As far as he was concerned everything was back to normal. Abby was confused.

Chapter Twenty-Two

When Abby found Yvonne in front of her store, her friend was wearing a surgical mask. Yvonne said, "I'm hoping wearing this thing will keep the smoke out of my lungs."

"I need to get me one. Where'd you get it?"

"The grocery store, but they ran out."

"Let's not talk out here. It's too smoky."

When they were inside My Things, Yvonne took off her mask and said, "So how'd it go?"

"Yesterday with Carl? Surprisingly well. We spent the day together, went for a hike, ate pizza at the Avalanche. I have to admit I felt comfortable with Carl. There's a stability to our relationship, a comfort level I'm used to that I like."

"What about last Sunday? Did you apologize?"

"I did. I said I was sorry for locking him out of the bedroom last Sunday. We slept together last night, but nothing happened. He fell asleep when I was in the shower. There's just no spark there, no electricity. Know what I mean?"

"I think so. Did you tell him about your engineer?"

"No, I didn't. Yvonne, I just couldn't bring myself to tell Carl about Tom. The only problem was he noticed my necklace and asked where I got it."

"And you said?"

"That I bought it at the Baker Park Jewelry Store. I couldn't tell him Tom gave it to me."

"So you lied to Carl."

"That's a little harsh, Yvonne. I wasn't lying – just withholding information."

"No. It was definitely a lie. You said you bought the necklace when it was Tom who bought it for you."

"Okay. You're right. You're making me feel guilty. I can't remember ever lying to Carl before. I'm not proud of it. I feel bad about it, but I just wasn't ready for a confrontation. Tom hasn't called since he left town. It's been five days now. I don't want to wreck my marriage just because I'm infatuated with someone. I don't know if I can count on Tom being here for me. Maybe I'll never see him again."

"He'll be back. And the train will be back. This fire won't last forever."

"Are you selling anything?"

"A couple of sales yesterday to local people."

"Your store appeals to everyone. I need the train to survive. Yesterday I had zero sales. Look at the sidewalk. It's empty."

"Kind of depressing."

"You can say that again. Guess I'll open up. Nothing better to do."

"Hang in there, girl."

Abby unlocked the Train Store. She went inside, turned on the lights and put the usual bills into the cash register. She had swept the floor the day before. With so little traffic on the street there was less dust in the store so she didn't need to sweep again. *Maybe less dust is the one bright spot in the whole wilderness fire catastrophe*, she thought. But the smoke in the air made up for it.

As she stood in front of her work table ruminating, the

phone rang.

"Silverton Train Store. This is Abby."

"Hi Abby." It was the familiar voice she had been waiting for. "It's Tom. How're you doing?"

"Oh, Tom! I'm so glad you called. I've been missing you so much. It's awful here without the train and without you. Physically I'm okay, but business is terrible. How are you?"

"I'm fine. I wanted to apologize for not keeping in touch. The train has furloughed most of us, so I took the opportunity to drive to Nebraska to see my mom. She's 92 and still living on her own. My dad died twenty years ago. I'm back in Durango. My sister is there to look after her, but I hadn't visited for a couple of months so I thought I'd better go."

"That's thoughtful of you. How's your mom

mentally? Does she have any sign of Alzheimer's?"

"Mentally she's fine, thank goodness. Physically she's still good, but she sits too much. She's losing muscle mass. I tried to take her for a walk, but we didn't get very far. She lives in the small town where I grew up. Everyone knows her. They take good care of her."

"I'm happy to hear that. Both my parents passed away. My mom had dementia the last years of her life. It was very difficult."

"You said business is bad?"

"Yes. Tourists can drive here from the north, but not the south. That makes us a cul-de-sac, a big dead end. If you come here and want to leave, you've got to drive back over Red Mountain where you just came from. Who wants to do that? Any news about the train?"

"That's what I'm calling about. The fire has moved west into the national forest, so the train tracks are no longer threatened and we're free to run. Two crews are coming up to Silverton tomorrow to bring the trains down to Durango. I'll be engineer on one of them. Don't think I'll have the opportunity to come over to the store, but thought I'd keep you informed about what's happening."

"That's the best news I've had since this whole thing began. When will the train resume its regular service?"

"We're aiming at starting up again this weekend with one train a day. Then hopefully we'll add a second train when people start making reservations again. So far the railroad has had to cancel 15,000 reservations. That's a huge financial hit."

"You're not kidding. I had zero sales yesterday. We're all suffering financially together. I'll keep an eye out for the D and S van tomorrow. If I see you're in town, I'll wave."

"Okay. I'll be happy to see you again."

"Me too, Tom. Thank you for calling."

"Bye."

Diary entry for 6-10-14: "Great news! Tom called. Crews are coming up tomorrow to take the trains back to Durango. Then they will start back up with a single train this weekend. I know our love was meant to be. Separation has been a struggle, but nothing can keep us apart."

Chapter Twenty-Three

With the Hermosa Cliffs Fire moving west, Highway 550 opened and tourists could once again drive north and south through Silverton. A few stopped to shop at the Train Store. Abby kept a close watch for the Durango and Silverton railroad vans bringing crews up to take the stranded trains back to Durango.

At 11:00 a.m. she heard two long whistles, the signal for the train to proceed. Abby was upset. She had missed the vans or they had turned on 12th Street and hadn't passed her store. There were two trains – only one had signaled it was starting to leave town. Maybe Tom was driving the other one.

Quickly, Abby put up her "Be Right Back" sign and locked the front door. She hurried down Greene Street and turned on 12th. One train had already left, but the other was still sitting on the tracks. The locomotive was at the far end of the train. She crossed Blair Street, running, holding onto her steam locomotive pendant with one hand, passing empty coaches as two long whistles sounded and the train jerked to a start. Sprinting, Abby caught up to the tender. She could see the back of the engineer's head as he leaned out of the cab.

"Tom! Darling!" Abby yelled. "Darling" just slipped out of her mouth. She didn't care who heard it.

When Abby drew parallel to the cab the engineer turned his head and looked down at her. It wasn't Tom. It was Bill North, one of the D and S veteran engineers. He had come in the store a few times.

"Hey Abby!" Bill shouted. "Tom's driving the first train. You just missed him."

Out of breath, Abby stopped and watched the train cars rumbling past her. *Dammit!* Her fists clenched as tears of frustration rolled down her cheeks. Walking back to Greene Street, she composed herself. *It's Thursday*, she thought. *Tom said the train should start this weekend. That will be Saturday. Maybe he'll be the engineer. Maybe I'll see him then.*

Yvonne was inside her store folding T-shirts. She noticed Abby's hair was disheveled. She was tucking her blouse into her jeans.

"Where've you been?" Yvonne asked.

"Crews came to take the trains back to Durango. Tom was one of the engineers. When I heard them leaving I went over to try to see him, but I was too late."

"You look a little bedraggled."

"I kind of made a fool of myself running to catch the second train after the first one left. Tom wasn't on it. He drove the first train."

"When are they starting service?"

173

"This weekend. One train on Saturday, then two whenever they get enough reservations. They've lost a lot of money."

"Tell me about it. So have I. I read in the paper that the economic losses in Durango and Silverton have gone into the millions of dollars."

"The train probably has insurance to cover this kind of situation. What about you? Do you carry insurance?"

"To cover damage to my merchandise from a fire or if the roof caves in, but not for the highway closing or the railroad stopping. I don't know if anyone offers that kind of insurance."

"If they do, it probably costs an arm and a leg."

Diary entry for 6-11-14: "Made an ass out of myself running after the train today. Didn't see Tom. Maybe Saturday."

Chapter Twenty-Four

Carl was waiting on a customer at Wheels Wings and Nautical Things when Stewart Sampson walked in. Stewart was proprietor of the Baker Park Jewelry Store in Silverton. When Carl finished with his customer, he greeted Stewart.

"Hey, buddy. Long time no see. What're you doing here?"

"Business has been so grim. I needed to get out of Silverton for a few hours. Left my wife in charge. How've you been doing?"

"My sales are down 25% since the fire started. Maybe not as bad as yours, but bad enough."

"We're down 50%. The smoke is gone and the train is supposed to start up again this weekend. Thank God."

"That's good news."

"How's Abby been doing at the Train Store?"

"She's down 50%, same as you. She loves that steam locomotive necklace you sold her."

Stewart paused. "I don't recall selling one of those to Abby. I did sell one to a locomotive engineer. New guy on the train."

"That's funny," Carl said. "I distinctly remember her saying she bought it from you."

"I guess you can ask her the next time you see her."

"Maybe I will."

After Stewart left, Carl pondered what his friend had told him. When Abby said she had bought the necklace for herself he thought it was a little odd, but she had bought other things for herself like her truck, so he just accepted what she said. He had no reason to think she wasn't telling the truth. Up until now he had always trusted Abby. He believed trust was the most important thing in a marriage. If you can't trust your wife, then who can you trust?

Chapter Twenty-Five

Tom didn't come to town that weekend. Neither did Carl. He called Abby Sunday morning. "Hey, Abby. I'm not coming to Silverton today."

"Oh. Why not?"

"I'm busy. Business has picked up. I lost so much the past couple of weeks I'm going to stay open today to see if I can make up for some of it. I'll see you later."

"Okay. I understand. Bye."

That's odd, Abby thought. Carl was a man of habit. He had driven from Ouray to Silverton on summer Sundays for as long as she could remember. She knew how much he loved their Sunday hikes together.

Had Abby been looking forward to seeing Carl? She didn't want to admit it. *I don't want to spend Sunday alone*, she thought. *Maybe I'll copy Carl's idea.* She opened the Train Store and made some money.

That afternoon, after the train left, Abby decided to drive over to Ouray to see Carl. When she came into his store he exclaimed, "Wow! This is a surprise. What brings you here?"

"I thought we could have dinner at Maxims." Maxims was an Italian restaurant.

"That's a good idea. Let me settle the credit card machine and get my totals from the cash register. What did you do today?"

"I decided to open the store. Like you said, maybe being open on Sunday can begin to make up for what I've lost the past few weeks."

"How did you do?"

"A couple of hundred bucks. Not bad."

"That's $200 you wouldn't have made if you weren't open."

Maxims was up Main Street from Wheels Wings and Nautical Things. It was a classic Italian eatery, dimly lit with red and white checkerboard table-cloths and candles dripping with wax stuck in empty wine bottles. Abby and Carl were early for supper. Just two other tables were occupied. Carl chose cannelloni and Abby ordered spaghetti with tomato sauce. They each asked for a glass of red wine. While they were waiting for their food, Carl said, "Stewart Sampson came in the other day."

An alarm went off in Abby's head. "Oh. What was he doing in Ouray?"

"Just escaping Silverton for a few hours." Carl's voice was calm. He leaned forward in his chair studying Abby's face. "He told me you didn't buy that steam locomotive necklace you're wearing. He said he sold one to an engineer on the train, but he didn't sell one to you. Didn't you tell me you bought it for yourself at his store?"

This was Abby's moment of truth. She sat back in her chair and took a deep breath. "Yes. I told you that, Carl."

The two were silent for a moment. The waiter came over to their table with a basket of garlic bread and their glasses of wine. Abby took a big swallow of her wine.

"So who's telling the truth? You or Stewart?"

"Stewart is."

"This is like pulling teeth. Where did you get the necklace?"

"The engineer gave it to me, Carl. He's new on the train. His name is Tom Walton. He's been coming in the store."

"Why would he do that? Give you a necklace."

"He likes me." Abby was looking down at the table cloth.

"Look at me! Jesus! He likes you? What's going on Abby?"

"I'm not sure. I think I've sort of fallen in love with him."

"Sort of fallen in love?" Carl's voice went up an octave. "What's that mean? You're supposed to be in love with me! I'm your husband, for God's sake!"

"It just happened. We haven't done anything."

The waiter brought their food.

Abby said, "I've lost my appetite. Can you put this in a box for me?"

"Do you want some garlic bread with your spaghetti?"

"Yes, please. That would be nice."

When the waiter left Carl exploded, "You haven't done anything?" A couple sitting at a nearby table stopped talking to listen. "That's just great! You mean you haven't slept with him yet?"

"Carl, please keep your voice down. No. I mean yes. That's what I mean. I haven't slept with him. You and I don't spend much time together, Carl. At least in the summer. Just Sundays. I get lonely."

"I don't like being separated either." Carl's voice was back to normal. He was speaking rapidly. "But that was our agreement. In fact, having two stores was your idea. You said we couldn't make ends meet with just the six-month income from the Train Store. So I started my store. Having two stores gives us enough income to make the payments on our house, pay our store rent for twelve months, pay our utilities and phone bills, make payments on your truck and have enough left over to do what we want in the winter. We agreed to see each other on Sundays. Jeez! I never thought our arrangement would wreck our marriage."

"I didn't either, Carl. That was never my intention. This thing − whatever it is − with Tom Walton just happened. I was bored and a little depressed."

The waiter brought Abby's doggy bag back to the table.

"So what happens now?" Carl asked. The couple at the next table leaned over toward Abby and Carl. "Do you want a divorce?"

"No, Carl. I don't know what I want." Abby got up

from the table. "I'm going back to Silverton."

Carl didn't get up when Abby walked out of the restaurant. He ate some garlic bread, half his cannelloni and drank his wine. Carl had already gone through one divorce. He didn't want to go through another. The first one was too painful. His children had sided with his first wife. He had lost touch with them. At least there were no children with Abby.

Sitting alone at the table, Carl felt humiliated, sick to his stomach. He didn't think he deserved this. What had he done wrong? He lived clean. He didn't drink excessively, he didn't do drugs, he didn't even smoke. He worked hard, he paid his bills on time, his wife had her own business. She even had her own damn truck. He didn't interfere with any of that. He loved his wife. He supported Abby. They were partners. Wasn't that what women wanted?

The waiter came over to Carl's table. "Sir, can I put

the rest of your cannelloni in a box for you?"

"Sure. Why not."

"And some garlic bread?"

"Sounds good. Thanks."

Driving back to Silverton, Abby pulled off the highway at the top of Red Mountain Pass. She couldn't see the road through her tears.

Chapter Twenty-Six

Tom came in the Train Store on Monday.

Abby dashed around her displays to cling to him.

"I can't stay," he said, wrapping his arms round her. "Just wanted to say hi."

She was sobbing.

"What's wrong? I thought you'd be happy to see me."

"I am. It's just…I've got a problem I have to solve."

Tom's brow furrowed. It saddened him not to be able to listen to Abby's problem. "Sorry I can't talk about it. Gotta get back to the train."

Abby clutched at Tom's sleeve with one hand while she wiped the tears from her face with the other.

"All right." She released her grip. "I'll let you go."

On Wednesday two trains brought tourists from Durango to Silverton. The day started off sunny, but around noon the sky darkened over the Animas River Canyon. Thunder and lightning crashed down over the San Juan Mountains and it began to rain. It was a heavy hard rain − a real soaker. Water dripped through small holes in the ceiling in the rear section of the Train Store building. No water leaked onto the framed railroad art in the front, but Abby felt a sense of dread as she waited fitfully for customers who never came.

The Hermosa Cliffs Fire had destroyed vegetation on a steep hillside above the tracks between Hermosa and the bridge over Highway 550. As often happens following wildfires in severe terrain, the rain that Wednesday caused a huge rockslide on the hill above the tracks. Boulders the size of small automobiles came crashing down, destroying the tracks and covering the highway with mud, rocks and debris for a half mile. Fortunately, both trains had passed over those tracks ten minutes before the rockslide came down. Had it hit the trains, hundreds of people would have been killed or injured.

A friend of Yvonne's lived in a condo near Hermosa just below the tracks. She saw the two trains go by. When the rocks started falling, she ran outside, got in her car and drove as fast as she could down Highway 550 toward Durango. When she was out of danger she phoned Yvonne to tell her what had happened. Yvonne told Abby.

"We only had the trains back for a few days," Yvonne said. "Now the tracks are demolished and the highway is closed again. What else can happen? Lightning striking the power station?"

"Don't say that," Abby said. "We've had enough bad luck. This summer's a disaster."

That evening Tom called.

"Hi. I guess you heard about what happened with the tracks."

"Yes. At least the trains got through before it happened. Does anyone know how long it will take to repair everything?"

"Not really. Maybe a month or longer. I've been furloughed again. As the last engineer hired, I'm the first to be let go."

"I'm sorry, Tom."

"Actually, it's come at a convenient time. My sister called and said my mom fell and broke her hip. I have to go back to Nebraska to help move her into a nursing home. She'll be bedridden. When her hip's healed she'll be in a wheel chair."

"I'm sorry to hear that."

"I tried to get her to exercise to build up her muscles, but she didn't want to. Breaking her hip has had a bad effect on her mind. My sister said she's losing it. She can't remember what she was just told. Guess it happens to the best of us. Medicare pays for Mom's hip surgery. I'll ave to sell her house to get the money to pay for the nursing home. That will take a while. I've got to go. I'll be in touch."

Abby had so much she wanted to say, but all that came out as Tom hung up was, "Bye."

Diary entry for 6-18-14: "Now I know why so many blues songs are associated with railroads – the K.C. Railroad Blues, the Mean Conductor Blues, the Frisco Whistle Blues. A train can bring happiness like the D and S did with Tom and me, but it can also bring heartbreak like the fire, this rockslide and now Tom is out of work and he's going back to Nebraska. What am I to do?"

Chapter Twenty-Seven

Business was slow in Ouray. Carl sat on a stool in his store deep in thought. What was he to do about Abby? He wasn't interested in looking for a lady friend to replace her − not for the time being. A checkout woman at the grocery store always had a warm smile for him, but he had a rule − one woman at a time. One was enough. Two or more would overwhelm him. Besides, he believed in the idea of marriage.

Carl wanted to try to save his marriage, but he knew it took two to tango. He didn't want to lose Abby. He knew he couldn't do any better than her, but if she had already decided their marriage was over there wasn't much he could do about it. One thing was certain. Carl wasn't a quitter. He was a fighter and he didn't give up easily. He had a plan that started with a phone call.

Abby had just put some lotion on her hands and was rubbing it in when the phone rang. She picked up the receiver carefully with the ends of two fingers. "Silverton Train Store. This is Abby."

Carl started their conversation normally. "Hi. It's me. How're you doing?"

"I guess I'm okay."

"Is this a good time to talk?"

"There's no one in the store right now. If I need to, I can talk and wait on someone at the same time."

"I heard about the rockslide."

"Just another disaster, but at least CDOT got busy right away and opened the highway."

"That's good news. Cause to celebrate."

"One thumb up."

"Any news of the train?"

"Just that the tracks and the roadbed were totally washed out for a mile above Hermosa. At least nobody got hurt, but the rocks and dirt invaded the condos between the tracks and the highway. People living there had to evacuate. The train is stuck in Durango. It'll take weeks to replace the tracks. They have to rebuild the roadbed and do something to reinforce the hillside so this doesn't happen again."

Carl shifted gears. "This thing with the engineer guy. Do you love him?"

"God, Carl. Don't ask me that."

"Do you love me?"

"It's too early in the morning, Carl."

"What kind of marriage do you want?"

"We don't make love very often."

"You're indifferent to me. You locked me out of the bedroom."

"That was just once."

"Once is enough."

"Do we need to go to marriage counseling?"

"We work all day every day in two separate towns. I don't think there are any marriage counselors in Ouray and there certainly aren't in Silverton. I went to marriage counseling with my first wife. It didn't work. The counselor was a guy, a pastor, who took my wife's side. He was a feminist."

"How can a guy be a feminist?"

I don't know. He was a male feminist supporter. I

don't think counseling is workable for us right now, we have businesses to run. Maybe this winter when we're not working. I've been thinking. There's no reason I can't run my store in Silverton. I've got a one year lease in Ouray that's over at the end of December. I'd just have to find a space in Silverton. It would bring us together. What do you think?"

"Can you make as much here as you do in Ouray?"

"That remains to be seen, but what do you say? I'm willing to do this if it will help save our marriage."

"Let's think about it."

"Is that the best you can do?" Carl's voice got louder. "You want to think about it? It's our marriage I'm talking about!"

"I've got some customers, Carl. I have to hang up."

Chapter Twenty-Eight

That afternoon, Abby found Yvonne closing her store.

"Do you have a minute?" Abby asked. "Are you going someplace?"

"This girl's got the disappearin railroad blues, but I'm all yours. What's happening?" She hung the "Closed" sign on her front door.

"That's funny. We're on the same page. I was thinking about trains and blues songs just yesterday. Carl called today."

"That's a plus. He wants to stay connected."

"He got right down to business, so to speak. Asked if I loved Tom and if I loved him, Carl."

"Yes. And…?"

"I didn't answer him directly on either of those questions."

"That's not exactly encouraging if you can't tell your husband you love him."

"It just took me by surprise. We don't normally engage in love talk."

"Maybe you should. I wanted to ask you something. I probably should have asked you this before. Do you and Carl complement each other? What I mean is, are your strengths and weaknesses balanced? Do you do something well that maybe Carl doesn't do so well and vice versa?"

"Well, yes. I guess so. I can be impulsive."

"Really? I'm being facetious."

"Yes, Yvonne. Didn't you know that? And he's more

careful. That works well in our businesses."

"What about Tom? Do you know him well enough to know his strengths and weaknesses?"

"No. We just met. We haven't had enough time together to find out if we complement each other. I just know I want to be around him. I need someone to connect to emotionally, someone to fill the emptiness I'm feeling."

"What I'm getting at is compatibility. Usually, incompatibility doesn't become obvious until after you're married, when you've settled down and you're going about your lives."

"You mean when the glow dies and the drudgery begins?"

"Abby! You've got to stop being so negative about your marriage. You haven't had to live through a divorce." Yvonne's eyes blazed. "Believe me! It's no picnic!"

"Calm down."

"Listen to me. Divorce is a personal failure. You don't realize it until it happens to you. At least, that's the way I felt. It shook me up. I haven't been able to have a normal, healthy relationship since my divorce. That was five years ago. "

"I'm sorry for you, Yvonne. I haven't made the decision to pull the plug on my marriage yet. Carl's still my husband, but there's something missing. Sometimes I think it's a confidence issue. I've never had enough confidence to go it alone – to be my own person."

"Maybe you don't realize it, but people, especially women, admire you for your business acumen. You have to be smart to run the Train Store alone like you do. That should give you confidence."

"Thanks, Yvonne. You're right. I love you." Abby gave Yvonne a big hug. "You always say the right thing. Doing well with the store should transfer to other parts of my life, but it doesn't seem to. Business is business, but like I said, I've got emotional needs that aren't being fulfilled."

"All right. Let me go. I can't talk anymore. Now that the highway is open, I'm going to Durango. I have some things to do there. I'll see you tomorrow."

Chapter Twenty-Nine

The next day Yvonne was sitting in front of her store with her eyes closed, feeling the warmth of the morning sun deep inside her. She was wearing a sleeveless turquoise cotton dress and waiting for Abby to come open the Train Store.

When Abby showed up, she said, "You look fabulous in that dress. The color goes great with the deep tan on your arms and face."

"Thanks. I've got a present for you." Yvonne handed Abby a paper bag from Walgreens.

"Is this what I think it is?" Abby tore the bag open. Inside was the photo Yvonne had taken of Tom Walton leaning out of the cab of the D & S engine enlarged to eight by ten inches.

Abby reached out and hugged her friend. "Thank you,

Yvonne. This is just what I wanted."

"Where will you put it?"

"I'm going to frame it and hang it up on the wall in the store across from the cash register so I can look at it all day long."

"What about Carl? He'll see it when he comes in."

"He'll just have to deal with it. It's my store."

"That's kind of cruel. Do you have a picture of Carl in the store?"

"No. Of course not. I don't need one. On second thought, if he objects, I can hang Tom's photo in my work room. Carl never goes there."

"I've got some other news for you," Yvonne said. Her lips were quivering with emotion.

"Business has been so bad with the train not coming and the highway shut down. I don't know if you heard, but the town has canceled the 4th of July fireworks due to the wildfire danger. The 4th has always been my best day of the year. I can't pay my store rent or the rent on my apartment anymore. I went to Durango yesterday to talk to an attorney about declaring bankruptcy. I'll have to shut down the store and leave town. I'm going to move in with my sister in Grand Junction."

Tears were streaming down Yvonne's cheeks. Abby threw her arms around Yvonne once more.

"No, Yvonne. You can't do this. We can work something out. I'll buy you a lottery ticket. I need you. You can live with me. Have you talked to your landlord?"

"Yes," Yvonne said, wiping the tears with her sleeve. "He can't help. His business isn't doing well either."

"Tell him you'll pay for two months next month."

"There's no guarantee when the train will start again. I'm liable for the rent payments on my lease. It doesn't run out until December. That's six months from now. I can't sublet the space. No one wants to open a business in Silverton if the train isn't running. I talked to my lawyer. If I declare bankruptcy I don't have to pay and my landlord can't sue me. It's unfair to my landlord, but that's what I have to do. You can't squeeze water out of a dry melon. I made a 'Going Out of Business' sign last night. I'll put it up today then I'm out of here at the end of the month.

Diary entry for 6-21-14: "I'm lost. My best friend is leaving town, my marriage is on the rocks, and the love of my life is in Nebraska. This is a bad time. At least I've got his picture on the wall."

Chapter Thirty

Sitting at her kitchen table the next morning drinking her coffee, watching the sun come up over Kendall Mountain, Abby did some thinking. What Yvonne had said two days ago about divorce being a personal failure had struck a chord with Abby. Carl was her husband – her chosen mate. Admitting she had made a bad decision when she agreed to marry Carl would be a blow to her pride. Abby had to make a choice – divorce Carl and see what happened with Tom Walton, or find a way to make her marriage work.

The train disasters happening one after the other were like date nails being pounded into the casket of Silverton's economy. Abby didn't know if or when she would see Tom Walton again. She needed someone to sustain her during those difficult times, someone she could depend on to be there for her. Yvonne announcing she was leaving removed Abby's main source of emotional support in Silverton.

Emotion and business mixed together in Abby's mind. She thought, *Yvonne closing My Things means a space is going to open next to the Train Store. Carl said he would like to move his business to Silverton so we could spend more time together. This is an opportunity for him to do so. Should I tell him Yvonne is closing her store? That would signal I want to stay married and my affair with Tom – if you could call it that – was just a fling, a spur of the moment dalliance, fun while it lasted, but over.*

She knew what she had to do. She reached for the phone and dialed Carl's number in Ouray. He picked up on the third ring.

Abby took a deep breath. "Hi. It's me. Are you busy?"

"No. Just dusting the shelves."

"It took you longer than usual to answer. I thought

you might have a customer."

"I was on the other side of the store. What's on your mind?"

"The other day you said you would be willing to move Wheels, Wings and Nautical Things to Silverton so we could be together more."

"Yes."

"Yvonne's quitting her store. The town has shut down the 4th of July fireworks. That's her biggest day of the season. Business has been so bad she can't pay her bills. That means the space next to the Train Store will be open next month and ready for occupancy. You could move in."

Carl paused before replying. His heart pounded in his chest. Caution, he told himself. "That's too bad. I mean about Yvonne. She's your best friend, isn't she?"

"I'm going to miss her a lot."

208

"Moving into her space is a great idea, but I've got my lease here. Breaking it would mean I'd have to pay my landlord six months rent while paying rent on the new space in Silverton. I can't afford that. And with the uncertainty about when the train will start running again, this isn't the greatest time to open a new business in town. Isn't there some way you can talk Yvonne into staying open? Beg her landlord to be patient? It's better to have someone in his space than to leave it empty, even if he's not getting his rent on time. The train will be back eventually."

"She's already talked to a lawyer in Durango. She's not happy about it, but she's going to declare bankruptcy so she doesn't have to honor the rest of her lease. I got the impression you wanted to relocate to Silverton as soon as possible."

"I do, but we've got to be practical about relocating. We can't afford to lose money on this deal or we'll wind up like Yvonne − bankrupt. Are there any other empty spaces in town?"

"None on Greene Street. That's where you need to have your store. Blair and the side streets aren't busy enough, except 12th and it's full. I'll talk to Yvonne again. I've got to go to work."

"Okay. Talk to you later."

Carl was going to say, "Love you," but Abby hung up too quickly. He felt good the rest of the day. He moved around the store with a spring in his step. Abby telling him about the empty store space meant she wanted him close to her so they could work on their marriage. That's what he wanted, but he needed to be cautious and not rush into anything. He wondered what had happened to her engineer.

Diary entry for 6-22-14: "First Carl tells me he wants to move back to Silverton. Then when a place for his store opens up he makes excuses for not returning to town. What's going on?"

Chapter Thirty-One

Two days later Carl called Abby. "Hi. You won't believe what's happened."

"Try me."

"Yesterday, a woman came in the store. We started talking and she told me she's looking for a space right here on Main Street in Ouray. She wants to open a business catering to dogs and their owners. Everything your dog needs – food, water bowls, leashes, shampoo. She's a licensed dog masseuse – she clips their nails, gives them baths. Anything and everything for dogs."

"Did you start sneezing when she came in the door?"

"No, why?"

"From your dog allergy."

"I forgot about that when she said she was looking for a space."

"I didn't know you needed a license to massage a dog."

"I didn't either. Maybe she took a class and when she graduated they gave her a license. Anyway, what do you think? If my landlord agrees to me subletting to this woman, I can be out of here by the end of the month. Is Yvonne's space still available?"

"As far as I know. She's been selling all her clothes at reduced prices. I bought an antique white lace blouse. I think you'll like it."

"I can't wait to see you in it. Can you contact her landlord for me? See if I can have her space."

"I'll do that right now. Talk to you soon."

"Okay."

"Carl wait, don't hang up. If this dog woman moves into your store space you won't be able to go back. Your allergy will kick in. You'll be coughing and sneezing."

"Haha. Hadn't thought of that. Guess it's the price I'll have to pay."

"Carl, I'm glad this is working out."

"Me too. Love you."

"Love you too. Bye."

Diary entry for 6-24-14. "Carl's moving his store back to Silverton. Told him I loved him. It wasn't hard to say. I feel relieved. Like a weight has been lifted from my shoulders."

Chapter Thirty-Two

That Sunday, Carl drove over Red Mountain Pass
early in the morning and came to the house. He carried
a package and an envelope. He found Abby sitting at
the breakfast table in her pink pajamas, socks, slippers
and bathrobe drinking coffee listening to the satellite TV
1970s music station. *A Whiter Shade of Pale* by Procol
Harum was playing.

"Hi. I've been waiting for you," Abby
said. She was not wearing her sterling
silver steam locomotive pendant necklace
gift from Tom Walton. It was locked in
her jewelry box – absent, but not
forgotten.

"Hi," Carl said. He leaned down to kiss Abby on the
cheek. She turned her head so their lips met and
lingered.

215

"Wow. That was nice," Carl said when he came up for air.

He handed Abby the package. "I brought you something."

Abby opened the paper wrapping. It was a box of chocolates. "Thank you, Carl. That's very thoughtful of you."

"I got them at the Russell Stover factory store in Montrose."

"Chocolate-covered cherries. My favorite. You remembered!"

Abby opened the box, took one of the candies and placed it in Carl's open mouth.

"You can have the first one."

He took her hand in his and licked the chocolate off her fingers.

They kissed again. Deeper this time.

Then Carl took a small box out of his pocket and opened it. Inside was the engagement ring he had given Abby fourteen years ago.

"I took your ring out of our safe deposit box at the bank. I want you to wear it."

He slipped the ring on her finger.

"It still fits," she said. "I'm surprised." Her voice was shaking. "My hands are so rough…"

"And here's something I wrote for you."

Carl gave Abby the envelope. Inside was a single piece of paper with a poem written on it. Abby read it out loud, her voice faltering.

For Abby from your husband

Now and again.
In a scented garden take me in your arms.
And wrap me in the warm caress of your love.

Now and again.
Touch me in a dream, your silky skin
Joined with mine, the movement ours.

Now and again.
Leave me full of the breath of you
And the certainty of your affection.

Now and again.
Make my heart joyous.
Let me show you the strength of my love.

Tears welled up in Abby's eyes. She reached out to
her husband. Carl knelt on the floor in front of her and

encircled his wife with his arms.

"Thank you, Carl. This is the most wonderful thing that's ever happened to me. It's like a brand new first date with my husband. Your poem is lovely. I didn't know you're a poet."

Carl looked into Abby's eyes. They were both trembling from the intensity of the emotion shared between them.

"I didn't either, until last night when I sat down and wrote it. I've never written anything before. The words just came pouring out of me. These feelings have been bottled up for a long time. Guess it took the crisis in our marriage to release them. I'm glad you like it."

"I love you, Carl."
"I love you too, Abby."

"Did you bring your clothes back from Ouray?"

"I packed a suitcase. It's in the car."

"Why don't you bring it in? On second thought – that can wait until we finish something we haven't done in a long time."

Reunited by Peaches and Herb was playing on satellite radio. Abby and Carl clung to each other.

"I missed your kiss," Carl whispered.

"It feels so good," Abby murmured.

They kissed passionately.

Final diary entry 7-1-14: "I was blessed to have Tom Walton in my life for a brief period of time. I will always hold in my heart the memory of his strength and tenderness, his love and laughter, but that relationship is in the past. I'm happy now, secure in the arms of my loving husband."

THE END

Robert Boeder divides his time between Thailand and Colorado. He is the author of two non-fiction books – *Beyond the Marathon. The Grand Slam of Trail Ultrarunning and Hardrock Fever. Running 100 Miles in Colorado's San Juan Mountains* and six novels – *The Chinese Laundry. A Novel of the San Juan Mountains, Silverton Burning, Zambezi River Bridge, Red Star Over Pattaya, The Crocodile's Tail,* and *Train Store Diary. Crocodile's Tail* is a sequel to *Red Star Over Pattaya.* All Boeder's books are available as paperbacks on amazon.com and ebooks on Kindle and other devices or by contacting the author directly through his website, www.robertboeder.com.

Made in the USA
San Bernardino, CA
25 July 2020

76079180R00136